The Kneebone Boy

ELLEN POTTER

SCHOLASTIC INC.
New York Toronto London Auckland
Sydney Mexico City New Delhi Hong Kong

ISBN 978-0-545-40409-9

12 11 10 9 8 7 6 5 4 3 2   11 12 13 14 15 16/0

Printed in the U.S.A.   40

First Scholastic printing, October 2011

Book design by Patrick Collins

For Adam and Ian, my happily ever after

Chapter 1

In which we meet the Hardscrabbles,
unearth a triceratops bone, and begin to like
Lucia even more

There were three of them. Otto was the oldest, and the oddest. Then there was Lucia, who wished something interesting would happen. Last of all was Max, who always thought he knew better. They lived in a small town in England called Little Tunks. There is no Big Tunks. One Tunks was more than enough for everyone. It was the most uninteresting town imaginable, except for the fact that the Such Fun Chewing Gum factory was on its west end, so that the air almost always smelled of peppermint. When the wind blew just right you could think you had been sucked down a tube of toothpaste.

I was the one voted to tell this story because I read the most novels, so I know how a story should be told. Plus I'm very observant and have a nice way of putting things; that's what my teacher Mr. Dupuis told me. I can't tell you which Hardscrabble I am—Otto, Lucia, or Max— because I've sworn on pain of torture not to. They said it's because the story belongs to all three of us, and I suppose they're right, but it seems unfair since I'm doing all the work. No one can stop you from guessing though.

The story will begin on a sparkling, sun-drenched afternoon in July. I think that's a good time to start because everything is so nice and pleasant at that time, with flowers blooming and birds singing and all that rubbish. You have to start nice and pleasant before you get to the more heart-thumping bits, in which the weather turns nasty and so do the people. And also, the story actually *did* start on a sparkling, sun-drenched afternoon in July, so I wouldn't be lying.

On a sparkling, sun-drenched afternoon in July, when the flowers were blooming and the birds were singing, Otto and Lucia were walking home from school arguing about what they were going to do when they grew up.

"We'll open up a tattoo parlour in Little Tunks," Otto said.

"Well, that's fine for you. *You'll* be the one drawing skeletons and tigers on people's bums," said Lucia, who incidentally looked exactly like her name. If you don't know what I mean, just picture long, thick, black hair that needs loads of shampoo to make a lather; a delicate, proud nose; and beneath two unapologetically thick eyebrows, dark eyes that were endlessly searching for something interesting to happen. If you think she sounds suspiciously heroine-like, be advised that she has flaws. She had a

2

terrible sense of direction, fought quite a lot with Max, and was on the short side.

"I won't tattoo bums," Otto said staunchly.

"You would if someone paid you loads of money," Lucia declared.

"Not even then," he said.

"Well . . . you would if the Queen came in and asked to have her bum tattooed," Lucia said, since she hated to lose an argument.

Otto and Lucia both silently contemplated this for a few moments.

"I might," Otto admitted, "just to say that I did."

Here's what Otto looked like, because I know you're going to wonder pretty soon: He was a tall, thin, slippery-jointed thirteen-year-old. His posture was appalling. His shoulders humped and his head drooped down, so that he always looked like he was up to no good. He had shiny, pale blond hair that always swung over his pale blue eyes. Wrapped twice around his neck was a long black cloth scarf embroidered with twisting oak leaves in silver thread. He wore the scarf all the time, in winter and summer. Even to bed. His front tooth was chipped, due to an incident in which he was up to no good.

The other very important thing you should know about Otto is that he didn't speak. I know I've already written that Otto spoke to Lucia, and it's not a lie really. He spoke with his hands, using a sign language that he and Lucia had devised long ago, after he suddenly stopped speaking at the age of eight. Their younger brother, Max, understood quite a bit of it, because he was fairly clever and extremely nosy; their father had tried very hard to decipher it but rarely could. The teachers never understood him at all but they didn't make a fuss over it. Truth be told, they were a little bit afraid of Otto. Most people in Little Tunks were.

From here on in, when I write "Otto said" you'll understand that he was signing the words with his hands. Lucia, on the other hand, usually spoke to him out loud. He could hear perfectly well, after all.

"And anyway," Lucia said, frowning, "what am *I* supposed to do at the tattoo parlour?"

"You can console the people who are crying and mop up the blood," Otto answered promptly.

"Oh, that's appealing." Lucia puffed out her nostrils. It was a lovely gesture of contempt that she used quite often. "And anyway, I don't think there's much blood involved if you do it properly."

They travelled through the narrow, winding streets, passing the brick terrace houses, the town park with its small pond and its three bad-tempered swans, and the sweet shop, which was owned by the Pakistani man who gave you back your change in little coin towers, the biggest coins on the bottom. Occasionally, they walked by other kids, also on their way home from school. The kids nodded at Otto and Lucia warily, but none of them stopped to toss them a friendly word, or even a filthy one. As a rule, no one in Little Tunks meddled with the Hardscrabble children. This was 75 percent due to the suspicious disappearance of their mother several years before, 20 percent due to the fact that the people in Little Tunks thought that the Hardscrabbles were strange, and 5 percent due to the Hardscrabble children—the two eldest, at least—being happiest in each other's company.

"Well, I say we buy a fully rigged ship and sail around the Pacific Rim. We'll navigate by the Orion constellation, and we'll search for people who've been shipwrecked on islands, then rescue them," Lucia said. (I'm beginning to think that you are pronouncing Lucia's name as though it were *Lucy* with an *a* at the end of it. That's wrong. You pronounce it Lu-CHEE-a. Say it a few times out loud and you'll forget about *Lucy-a*.)

"You won't need to navigate by the Orion constellation," Otto said. "You can use radar equipment."

"Yes, but maybe I'll *choose* to navigate by the Orion constellation."

"And people generally don't get shipwrecked on desert islands anymore," Otto said.

"I *know* that," Lucia said, her nostrils puffing again, although not very widely since she hadn't really thought of that. "But back in the old days, ladies travelled on those ships sometimes. If they got shipwrecked on an island with everyone else, don't you think they might eventually have children? And then their children might have children, and then there might be a whole pack of them by now, living on seaweed and mud, just waiting for someone to come rescue them. Imagine how excited they'd be to see our white sails fluttering on the horizon." Lucia's glittering black eyes were now fixed on the horizon of Little Tunks, which consisted of some grimy terrace-house roofs, the Such Fun Chewing Gum factory's chimneys pumping out peppermint smoke, and a cow pasture beyond that. "After we rescued them, we'd be on all the telly news shows and they'd put up plaques about us on park benches."

She glanced over at Otto. He'd shoved his hands in his pockets and looked markedly unimpressed. She frowned, considered, then added, "Of course, it's likely that there'd be some strange deformities among the stranded people. Inbreeding being such a problem."

Beneath his overgrown hair, his pale, interested eyes slid toward his sister. "What kind of deformities?"

"Oh, children with hair growing on their faces, people with twelve toes. Like that."

Otto was an avid collector of the strange and unusual. In fact, he hoped one day to open a museum of abnormalities right in Little Tunks, but he needed to enlarge his collection first. Thus far, he owned three specimens: a two-headed cornsnake; a one-eyed frog; and a lobster with an extra claw on one side, all of which he'd purchased from a catalogue.

"Well," Otto said, "that's all right then. But I still think a tattoo parlour is better."

Suddenly Otto stopped walking. His body stiffened and his hand reflexively yanked his scarf tighter around his neck, something he always did when he was nervous. Lucia looked at him questioningly, then followed his gaze across

6

the street. A thin woman with a cap of thick grey hair was prodding at a small object on the sidewalk with a stick.

"Oh, for heaven's sake!" Lucia hissed. She grabbed Otto by the elbow and quickened their pace. But it was no use. Mrs. Carnival had spotted them.

"Hoo! Hoo, Hardscrabbles!" Mrs. Carnival called to them, waving her stick.

Ignoring her was no good, they knew. They had tried it before. She would hunt them down clear across town if need be.

Reluctantly, they crossed the road while Mrs. Carnival waited, tapping the stick against the pavement. Her eyes, which were the exact color of bananas when they go thoroughly rotten, fixed on them impatiently.

"Come on, don't drag your feet, Hardscrabbles! Stand up straight, Otto, I've told you a hundred times not to walk like a baboon. You may act the part of the village idiot but there's no need to walk like one!"

Lucia opened her mouth to shoot back an angry response, but Otto stopped her with a quick shake of his head. He was right, of course. It was no use arguing with Mrs. Carnival. She would always have the last word, and besides, they had to stay at her home several times a year. It wasn't a good idea to get on her bad side.

As Lucia and Otto came close, Mrs. Carnival turned her attention back to the object on the ground.

"Get rid of this thing," she demanded, nudging it distastefully with the tip of her stick. "I don't want to touch it, and it's spoiling the street."

7

It was a robin, tiny and plump and lying horribly still. Otto knelt down next to it. Its thin eyelids were closed except for the tiniest slit, through which a still-bright dark eye gleamed.

Otto shook his hair to the side in order to see better, and with one finger he gently touched the bird's small russet chest.

"Is it dead?" Lucia asked Otto.

He shook his head no.

"Well, it *should* be if it had any sense! Flew into my window, the nitwit," Mrs. Carnival said. "What are you doing down there, Otto? I asked you to get rid of it, not groom it! Oh, get out of the way, I'll kill it myself." And she lifted her stick in order to bring the pointed end down on the little bird's chest.

Swiftly, Otto slid his hand beneath the little bird and scooped it up before Mrs. Carnival could touch it. He wrapped his scarf around it gently and cradled it against his chest.

"Ridiculous boy," Mrs. Carnival muttered, shaking her head. "Remember to wash that scarf afterwards," she called to Otto as he and Lucia walked away. "That bird is certainly diseased. I won't have you staying at my house if you catch something from it."

"As though that's punishment," Lucia said, almost loud enough for Mrs. Carnival to hear. But not quite. Mrs. Carnival was the only person who was willing to take care of them when their father went on his trips abroad. The Hardscrabbles didn't like her but they needed her.

Or Dad felt they did anyway, though I'm sure they were perfectly capable of taking care of themselves.

Otto cupped his hand over the small lump under his scarf as he and Lucia passed through the heart of town and then turned up a lonely street whose broken pavement tilted this way and that. On either side of the road were a few houses in moderate states of disrepair. Their own house was at the very end of the street, a ramshackle butter yellow house with a wild-looking garden in the front. Ruffled pink and white roses spilled giddily every which way, blue lobelia carpeted the ground, and gangly lilies stretched up toward the sun, their lemon-colored petals unfurled. Arched over the brick path leading toward the house was a rickety arbour that was thatched with bright purple clematis.

A black-and-white cat named Esmeralda was sunning herself on the path, but when she saw Otto and Lucia approaching she popped up and bolted out of the garden and across the road. She wasn't their cat anyway. She was only one of the many street cats that hung around their house. The cats came when their mother had still lived with them and they still kept coming after she was gone. Their mother didn't believe in keeping animals, Dad told them, any more than she believed in keeping humans. Creatures stayed as long as they needed to stay, she had said, and when it was time for them to leave, you just had to tip your hat and wish them well.

Ironically, though, the cats *never* thought it was time to leave the Hardscrabble house. It was really as if they were hanging around waiting for Tess Hardscrabble to return. Consequently, as Lucia and Otto approached the house, they startled six other cats out of the depths of the garden. A seventh, a big fat tabby, had draped itself in front of the door and would not move, so they had to step over him.

Inside the hallway, Otto and Lucia dropped their schoolbags and headed directly to the kitchen, just as they always did, but they stopped short at the entrance. Sitting at the kitchen table was a chubby red-haired girl they'd never seen before. In front of her was a large bowl, into which their younger brother, Max, was scooping chocolate ice cream from the carton. He stopped when he saw Otto and Lucia, and his face grew a little pink.

"Who's this?" Lucia demanded.

"Her name is Brenda. She's new at school, moved here all the way from Loughborough, and doesn't know a soul, so I thought wouldn't it be a good thing for her to come over." Max said this very quickly, and there was a pointed tone to his voice when he said that Brenda was *new at school*.

What followed was a long awkward silence, during which Otto slouched even more than usual and cradled the robin closer to his chest. Lucia flashed an irritated glance towards Max then turned her dark eyes on Brenda. Her expression was stern but kind.

"Did Max tell you that he has a time machine in the basement?" Lucia asked Brenda.

The girl shook her head while Max hastily plopped another scoop of ice cream in her bowl.

"Did he tell you he has a pair of llamas in the backyard?" Lucia persisted.

Brenda shook her head, but her eyes flitted to the window that faced the backyard.

"No, Brenda, there aren't any llamas there," Lucia said. "Nor time machines. Nor anything else that Max might have told you. Incidentally, what *did* he tell you to make you come here?"

Brenda looked down at her bowl of ice cream wistfully, as though she sensed that she was not going to have a chance to eat it.

"Why don't you mind your own business, Lucia," Max said, scooping out the last bit of ice cream from the container.

Lucia ignored him and kept her black eyes on Brenda, who was beginning to squirm. "Well?" Lucia demanded.

"He told me he'd found a brontosaurus bone in the garden," Brenda said. Then she looked at Max. "Was that a lie?"

Lucia snorted. "Oh, for goodness' sake, of course it was a lie! I'm surprised a girl your age would believe such rubbish. I honestly think kids are getting stupider by the year." She murmured this last bit to Otto.

Brenda frowned over at Max, who quickly turned his back to grab a container of milk from the fridge.

"Can I eat the ice cream, at least?" Brenda asked Lucia.

"You don't have to ask *her* permission, you know," Max said, placing a glass of milk in front of Brenda. "She's not the parent."

The real, actual parent walked into the kitchen just then. He didn't look much like a real, actual parent. Casper Hardscrabble was a tall, thin, bespectacled man with curly dark hair down to the base of his neck and a grizzled, unshaven face. His eyebrows were thick, like Lucia's, but his were the scowling type. Had he plucked them, he might have looked more friendly to his neighbours. He would have resembled a shy, rumpled college professor, and his neighbours might not have thought the awful things that they thought about him. But he wasn't the type to pluck them, so there's nothing to talk about really.

Oh, and he was wearing yellow pyjamas.

"You're new," Casper said to Brenda.

"She was Max's idea," Lucia muttered.

Casper looked at Brenda's bowl of ice cream, then at his youngest child, who was now sitting across from Brenda, pretending to be engrossed in smashing the lumps of sugar in the sugar bowl with the back of a spoon.

"I see you've finished off the ice cream," Casper said, glancing at the empty ice cream carton on the kitchen counter.

Brenda squirmed a little.

"Well done," Casper said. "I was just about to throw it out to make room for the triceratops bone."

They all looked at him with puzzled expressions.

"What?" he said, gazing back at them. "You have to put dinosaur bones *some*where before the museum comes to fetch them, don't you? A freezer is the best place. Keeps them nice and fresh."

"You never said anything about having a dinosaur bone, Dad." Lucia narrowed her eyes at him.

"Not to you, maybe," Casper said. "But I told Max all about it this morning, didn't I?"

Max stared at him for a moment, then nodded.

"Really? Then why did he tell Brenda it was a bronto-saurus bone?" Lucia persisted.

"Well, that's what I thought it was at first," Casper said. "But I looked it up afterwards. It's definitely triceratops."

"Can I see it?" Brenda asked, already making a fair-sized dent in her ice cream.

"Oh, yes, let's *all* see it," Lucia said, throwing a dry look at Max, who had wilted in his chair.

"All right. Wait right here. I'll go get it." Casper opened the kitchen door and walked out into the garden. All the kids went to the window to watch what he would do next.

"My dad is never home at this hour," Brenda said. "Doesn't your dad work?"

"Sure, he does. He just works at home," Max explained. "And every so often he goes away."

"Where?" Brenda asked.

Casper was now circling the garden in his bare feet, staring hard at the ground.

"All different places. The Philippines, Africa, Indonesia," Max said. "He paints portraits of kings and queens and empresses. Not the famous ones, though. The ones he paints have been booted off their thrones."

Brenda scrutinized him doubtfully, then turned to Lucia. "Is he lying?"

"No, he's actually telling the truth this time," Lucia replied distractedly, her eyes fixed on her father. Casper was kneeling down, frog fashion, and was clawing up the earth. It flew backwards between his legs.

"Do you get to go with him?" Brenda asked.

Max shook his head. "He's too busy when he's there to look after us. And we'd miss too much school." He added in a grim voice, "We stay with a lady in town."

"What about your mum?" Brenda asked, looking around suddenly as though their mum might be hiding in the room somewhere.

"Haven't you heard about our mum?" Lucia asked.

Brenda shook her head.

Max flashed a warning look at his sister, which Lucia completely ignored.

"She's dead," Lucia said.

"She's gone missing," said Max.

"Dead," Lucia said.

"Missing," Max said. "Dad says she's missing."

"He just says that to make us feel better. She's dead."

Now Brenda appeared completely confused. Her eyes darted around nervously between Lucia and Max, stopping briefly to look at Otto, who would not look back at her.

A scurrying movement out the window made them turn their attention to Casper again. He was down on all fours, one hand pawing around the hole he'd dug in the ground. He pulled something out, something largish, and began brushing the dirt off of it. Then he hopped up very nimbly and trotted back to the house. The front of his pyjamas was filthy and there were bits of soil in his hair and on his spectacles, but when he entered the kitchen, he held up the dirt-encrusted object triumphantly.

"Found it!" he cried. "I put it back in the ground earlier, just until I could get the freezer cleaned out."

He placed the thing on the kitchen table with a thump. It was definitely a bone, and a very large one.

"Whoa," Brenda said quietly.

"Max believes it may be the beast's ankle bone," Casper said, looking at his son admiringly. Brenda did the same, and Max's face turned bright red.

"Oh, for goodness' sakes, that's just an old beef bone," Lucia said. "One of the neighbourhood dogs probably buried it."

"Really?" Casper raised one eyebrow at Lucia, a thing that none of his children could do, though they all had practiced in front of a mirror. "Are you sure?"

"Yes," Lucia said resolutely.

"How much do you want to wager?" Casper asked.

Lucia shrugged carelessly but she looked a little uncomfortable.

"How about your birthday money?" Casper suggested.

Lucia hesitated while Otto examined the bone with his free hand, as though he were trying to assess Lucia's odds.

"Forget it." Lucia backed down. Her nostrils puffed

out very widely and she added smirkily, "Believe what you want to believe."

"Well said!" Casper exclaimed and he kissed Lucia's forehead, leaving a smudge of garden dirt on it.

Later, Lucia watched out the window as Max walked Brenda down the front path, then stood at the edge of the front lawn and watched her walk away. Brenda turned around once to look back at him and he waved enthusiastically. She waved back. A small careless wave.

Here's what Max looks like: dark hair like Lucia and blue eyes like Otto. Chin slightly cleft like Lucia and nose on the snubby side like Otto. If you studied him, you would swear he looked like a perfect combination of the two, but if you looked away from him suddenly and then you looked back at him, you'd think that he didn't look a single thing like either of them.

"He thinks she's going to come back," Lucia murmured.

Otto looked up from the robin, confused for a moment, then followed Lucia's gaze out the window.

"Brenda will go to school tomorrow and tell everyone about the dinosaur bone," Lucia continued airily, "and everyone will tell *her* about Mum. Then Brenda won't ever step foot in this house again."

Here is what happened to their mum. One day she was gone. Casper looked everywhere for her. The police looked everywhere for her. The police searched their house too, and they brought dogs to sniff through the garden, as though Casper had done something fiendish, you understand. A crowd of neighbours stood outside, watching. In the end, the dogs found exactly nothing, but you can't have dogs sniffing through your garden to find your missing mum without there being some serious damage to your family's reputation. Mum was never found. Soon after that, Otto started wearing his scarf all the time.

Here is the part I hate to even mention, but since it figures into this story you'd better hear it now. An ugly rumor started going around. People whispered that Otto had strangled his mum with that very scarf in a fit of rage, and that Casper had buried his wife in the yard to cover for him. Otto had always been a strange, quiet boy. Strange, quiet boys are never popular in small towns. Kids in school started harassing Otto with questions about what he'd done to his mum and where her body was buried and did her ghost haunt him at night until, quite suddenly, Otto simply stopped talking. He'd never talked much to begin with, so it was just a stone's throw to nothing at all. Still, that made things even worse, of course. Before long, all of Little Tunks acted as if the Hardscrabbles had the lurgies, which in case you don't know is what kids say you have when they don't want anything to do with you, as in "Ewww, don't touch the Hardscrabbles, they have the lurgies!"

"Don't you think we should warn Max?" Otto asked. "So he won't get his hopes up about Brenda coming back?"

Lucia stared at her younger brother, who was now walking toward the huge oak tree by their house, which he would certainly climb to sit on his usual rooftop perch by the chimney. His stride was bouncy and his eyes were lost in some imagined future that was clearly much brighter than the present.

"No. Let him believe what he wants to believe," Lucia said. Her voice didn't sound smirky this time. It sounded full of genuine pity. Which should make you like her even more.

Chapter 2

In which Otto finds something interesting,
Lucia listens to nothing at all,
and more stuff happens

The little robin stayed wrapped in Otto's scarf throughout dinner, perfectly motionless except for its tiny chest,
which rose and fell with rapid breaths. Toward the end of
dinner, though, the bird began to twitch. It lifted its head,
then attempted to right itself, its claws scratching at the
scarf to gain a grip.

"I think it's coming round," Otto said, gazing down
at it.

Casper looked over at Otto through his thick round
spectacles, then at Lucia.

"What did he say?" Casper asked her.

"He says it's coming round," Max interjected. He took
every opportunity to show that he knew Otto's language
as well as Lucia did.

"What is?" Casper asked.

19

"A bird, Dad," Lucia said. "Otto's got a bird in his scarf."

"Ah," Casper said, and went back to his dinner. He saw so many odd things in his line of work that a bird in a scarf at dinner was fairly ordinary.

"Oh, poor thing," Lucia said, watching while Otto carefully disentangled the pinny little claw from the scarf. "We should put it in a box. Just until we're sure it's fine."

So off they went to search for a spare box. You always think there is an endless supply of spare boxes, but there never really is. The spare ones are nearly always smashed or else have a mouse corpse curled in the corner. There were no spare boxes to be found in the basement or in any of the closets and the poor little robin was beginning to really make a fuss.

"We might try Dad's studio," Otto suggested.

That hadn't occurred to Lucia. Casper's attic studio always seemed like its own separate flat that coincidentally happened to be attached to the top of their house. They opened the door at the far end of the upstairs hallway and climbed the steep, narrow stairs, right away smelling the nutty odor of linseed oil and, lurking behind that, the nostril-wincing sting of turpentine.

They didn't often enter Casper's studio when he was in there. The room wasn't off-limits exactly; it was just that Casper acted differently while he was at work in his studio. He stared at his sketch pad when he spoke to his kids. His voice grew vague, and his eyes had a faraway cast. In the studio, Casper's children felt slightly less substantial, as though they were one of Casper's daydreams, that

20

might grow fuzzy around the edges and vanish without warning.

When Casper wasn't in the studio, though, the children did like to come in to see the sketches hanging on the wall. They were the sketches that Casper brought home from his travels abroad—sketches of princesses and sultans, barons and kings, and an occasional knight (the actual paintings were left with his clients, of course, but Casper was able to take home the preliminary sketches).

In fairy tales, kings and princesses always look different from the everyday person. They're better looking or taller or fatter or even uglier. You'd think that was just all nonsense in real life, since royals are just people like everyone else.

Except, they're not.

They really do look different from the average person, even royalty who have been booted off the throne or have lost all their money. Casper's sketches proved it.

The Duchess of Hildenhausen, for instance, was a thick-jawed, middle-aged woman with long blond ringlets that were spiked with tiny cornflowers. One of her huge blue eyes went the wrong way, so that she looked just like a doll that had been rattled about by an angry child. And there was Prince Wiri, who had ruled The Sister's Islands in the South Pacific until his family was accused of witchcraft and they were exiled to Fiji. The black-haired Prince Wiri, dressed in a white military uniform crowded with epaulets, was an exceptionally handsome young man—as handsome as any movie star—but he would not smile or even show a hint of happy in any of Casper's sketches. Lucia enjoyed feeling sorry for him. Then there was the immensely fat Prince Andrei, whose family had once ruled a small principality south of Bulgaria. He had squinty eyes and a long, thin black beard, frayed on the ends. Perched on his shoulder was a black fox. Casper said that the fox was very clever and could bounce on a tiny trampoline that Prince Andrei had had built for him. Still, the fox didn't like Casper and would occasionally leap off the prince's shoulder to vomit on Casper's shoe.

Ex-royals were more difficult than regular people too. Casper said this was because they were frustrated. A duchess who lives in a tiny four-storey walk-up with a leaky toilet will never be a happy duchess, he said. They snipped and snapped and did strange things. While painting the Duchess of Hildenhausen—the lady with the wonky eye—Casper was interrupted dozens of times while the duchess leapt up to throw boiled potatoes at a mouse that she swore had been harassing her for months.

Also, unlike regular people, royalty didn't feel the need to pay their bills. Once in a great while they paid Casper what they said they were going to pay him. But more often than not Casper would come away with little more than partial payment, a box of expensive chocolates, and a promise of payment in full when their "affairs were settled" or "after the sale of a house in Spain." Ex-royals, it turned out, were a pretty shifty lot.

So Casper supplemented his income by doing

illustrations for small kitchen appliance repair manuals and occasionally for the *Journal of British Hog Farming.*

"Why don't you just paint regular people, Dad?" Max had once asked him. "At least they'd pay their bill."

"Probably," Casper said. "But there is something extraordinary about the face of a person who has fallen from greatness. They remind me of angels tossed out of heaven who are now struggling to manage the coin-operated washing machine at the Scrubbly-Bubbly Laundromat."

You must make allowances for artists like Casper. They get romantic ideas about things.

There were plenty of boxes in the studio crowded into the low corner of the attic, but they were all filled. Some contained bundles of old sketch pads and others had loose drawings and still others held copies of toaster repair manuals that Casper had illustrated or back issues of the *Journal of British Hog Farming.*

"Here," Lucia said, picking out a small carton from the back and handing it to Otto. "This one's not full yet. We could just shift some of the papers inside to another box and free it up."

Otto put the box down and looked inside. "I think it's just garbage in here. See, most of it's crumpled."

"Well, no wonder," Lucia said, walking over to Casper's dustbin. The dustbin was heaped up high with papers. Bits of pencil shavings were spilling off the top of the heap and had pooled around it on the floor. Lucia scooped up the shavings and tucked them in the corner of the dustbin, then shoved the rubbish down with the heel of her hand.

"Honestly, this place is beginning to look as wild as the garden," she said, lifting up the dustbin. "I'll go empty this downstairs."

And while she did, Otto found something interesting in the box of crumpled things.

This isn't surprising. Otto was very good at finding things that were not meant to be found. He often found birds' nests tucked in bushes. Once he found a litter of kittens that Esmeralda had stashed beneath a loose floorboard in the garden shed—two white ones and a little black one. Last year he found a bunch of love letters that Casper had written to their mum. They were shoved in the pocket of her dressing gown, which was shoved in the back of Casper's closet, along with all her other clothes. The clothes still smelled of peppermint from the Such Fun Chewing Gum factory.

What *is* surprising, however, is that Otto didn't tell Lucia he had found the interesting thing in the box. He usually told Lucia everything. By the time she returned he had tucked the interesting thing in his back pocket, and all Lucia saw was a robin standing upright in an empty carton and Otto looking slightly paler than usual.

(I hope you don't think I'm teasing by not telling you what Otto found. I will, I promise. It's just that there is a right time and place for everything, and 7:19 p.m. on a Thursday in Casper's attic studio is simply not the right time and place.)

◆ ◆ ◆

That night, Lucia lay in her bed, listening to nothing. The sound of nothing is the most ominous sound in the world. It's the sound a cat makes a second before it lunges for a mouse and sinks its arrow-tippy teeth into the poor thing's neck. The sound of nothing was also the sound that Casper made right before he was about to leave them.

Usually, Casper was a night owl. The darker it grew, the busier he became. He cooked at night, he painted at night. His children went to sleep to the lullaby of the radio that he played in his studio or his quick footsteps creaking through the house until the wee hours of morning. But right before Casper was to leave for a job, he slept. Perhaps it was anxiety that tired him out. Or excitement.

But he hadn't mentioned a new job, Lucia thought. And he'd been away just two months before. Surely he wouldn't make them stay with Mrs. Carnival again so soon?

To take her mind off the sound of nothing, Lucia did what she always did when she felt troubled. She stared at the Sultan of Juwi. She had strategically hung him above her dresser, directly across from her bed, so she could gaze at his face before she went to sleep and wake up to the sight of it in the morning. The white-robed sultan sat in the center of a fountain, on the head of a stone cherub that poured water out of a jug. The sultan held an egg in one hand and a silver demitasse in the other while he looked directly out at Lucia. She knew his face by heart: the creamy skin, the flat disk of cheekbone, the amused wide-set dark eyes that seemed to see all her worst qualities and like her even more because of them. Perched on his head was a crown that looked like a large bejewelled mustard lid, and his white robe was cinched around the middle with a black sash. The left ear had a small hoop earring in it, and the right ear was a bit mangled looking. A mischievous half smile curled one side of his mouth. It was the smile of someone who has recently made a prank phone call. When Lucia told her father that, Casper nodded.

"Quite possible, knowing the sultan." Then Casper's face grew sad, as did Lucia's, because they were both thinking about the awful thing that had happened to the sultan shortly after the sketch was done.

I'm going to tell you the story of the Sultan of Juwi now, even though my English teacher, Mr. Dupuis, says it's bad form to skip back and forth in time. He says that just confuses readers. So I'm giving you fair warning that I'm going to be doing it in a moment, and if you're still confused I don't know what to say except you may be slightly daft.

It was two years ago. Casper had just returned from a trip to the Juwi Islands, off the coast of Indonesia, and he was unpacking his sketches from his leather portfolio and laying them out on the kitchen table for his children to look at. This was something he did every time he returned from one of his trips. The Hardscrabble children all loved to see his sketches and to hear stories about the people he had painted. Casper would tell them about the silly things his clients said and the absurd things they did. He found them amusing but ridiculous, which pleased his children. If you think about it, you can see why. Casper left his children to be with them, so in a way they were the children's competition.

But when he unpacked the sketch of a handsome boy with a half smile on his face, Casper's face turned grim. Hastily, he tried to stuff the sketch back into his portfolio.

"Wait," Lucia said, putting a hand on the sketch. "Who's that?"

Casper sighed. "The young Sultan of Juwi."

"Sultan?" Lucia said, staring hard at the picture. "I always imagined a sultan would look more . . . I don't know, swarthy-ish."

"His mother was an American, I think," Casper said.

"Was? Is she dead?" Lucia asked.

"Extremely," Casper said. "So are his father and his sister and three brothers."

"How?" Lucia asked.

"Awful story really. It happened when the sultan, at that time just a prince, was fifteen years old. A fountain had been erected in the village square, and the royal family was to do the honor of unveiling it. What they didn't know was that the prince's own uncle had been plotting against the royal family. A fellow named Azziz, a doctor, well educated—Oxford, if I remember correctly—and power hungry. Now he had the perfect opportunity to wipe out the whole royal family in a single day. Just as the young prince's father removed the cloth from the fountain, the royal family was ambushed and murdered, even the youngest, a girl who was only two. They say that the fountain's water turned red that day, dyed with the royal family's blood. They would have killed the young prince as well, but he was home that day, ill with the flu. So here he was, age fifteen—just two years older than you, Otto, imagine!—and he was crowned the new Sultan of Juwi. He had four advisors, all wise and good. They worried that Azziz would try and kill him too, and they urged him not to leave the palace, and to duck when he passed a window, in case a sniper was waiting outside. But the sultan couldn't live like that. He was too bold, too interested in life. The day after he was crowned, the young sultan told everyone, 'If I die this morning, remember to feed my pet peacock.' And off he went to eat his lunch at the very fountain where his family had just been killed."

"Mental," Otto said.

"Maybe. Some people say that madmen are protected by the gods." Casper smoothed Otto's hair away from his left eye. "So are the fearless."

"Anyway," Casper continued, "every day the young sultan went to the fountain to eat his lunch, wearing a black sash around his waist to show that he was still in mourning for his family. He refused to take his bodyguards, and always reminded his servants, 'If I die today, remember to feed my pet peacock.' Then he walked to the village square alone, stepped right into the fountain, water and all, and climbed to the tippy-top of it. From his robe pocket, he pulled out a hard-boiled egg and he nibbled on it between sips of tea from a silver demitasse.

"The people in his village were so touched by the young sultan's bravery that they began to come to the fountain and eat lunch with him. Soon nearly the entire village would arrive with their bowls of boiled rice and onions and their flasks of strong coffee and they surrounded the young sultan as he ate his egg. He couldn't have asked for a more devoted army. Dr. Azziz would have loved to kill the boy at the fountain, since the young sultan was the only person standing between him and the throne. But Dr. Azziz was afraid that if he killed the sultan, it would cause an instant rebellion among the people. They loved him that much."

The Hardscrabbles all looked at the drawing again. The sultan smiled back at them so mischievously that they couldn't even be jealous of the way Casper felt about him.

"What's wrong with his ear?" Max asked.

"His ear? What do you mean?" Casper said.

Max leaned across the table and pointed at the mangled right ear.

"Ah!" Casper said. "Nothing was wrong with it. It's just that the sultan vanished before I could finish the sketch."

"Vanished? He was finally killed at the fountain, do you mean?" Lucia said, suddenly feeling sickish in her gut.

"No, not at the fountain. No, the cowards who took him did it in the middle of the night. No one heard a sound. In the morning, the only thing his advisors found in his room was an empty bed and the black mourning sash lying on the floor, stomped on by muddy boots."

"Where did they take him?" Lucia asked.

"No one knows." Casper shrugged one shoulder.

"Do you think they killed him?" Lucia asked.

"Of course they did," Max said.

Casper looked out the window, gazing at the wild garden for a few seconds before swallowing hard. He picked up the drawing of the sultan and began to tuck it back into his portfolio.

"Can I have it, Dad?" Lucia asked.

"What, the sketch? But it's no good really. It's not finished."

"I don't care. I like it," Lucia said.

She hung it on her wall.

But tonight, even the sight of the Sultan of Juwi couldn't distract Lucia from the terrible silence (and now we are back to the present. See, that wasn't confusing, was it?). She slipped out of bed, wrapped herself in her dressing gown, and went down the hall to the boys' room. Max was sound asleep on the top bunk, his blankets thrown off of him as usual and his foot dangling from the edge of the bed. Otto was stretched out on the bottom bunk, his hands folded above the blankets, his eyes wide-open. The box with the robin inside it was next to his bed, one of Otto's old T-shirts partially covering the top.

As Lucia approached, Otto slowly turned his head towards her as though he'd been expecting her. He wore a pair of pyjamas made of purple silk, heavily embroidered with red dragons, which Casper had brought back from China. And of course, he wore his scarf.

Lucia peered at the robin in the box before she sat down on the edge of Otto's bed. "He looks much better," she whispered.

Otto nodded. "I'll probably let him go in the morning."

They were silent for a moment before Lucia whispered ominously, "Dad's sleeping."

"I know," Otto answered.

"But it's too soon! He only just got back from Africa."

"That was months ago," Otto said.

"Still, it's sooner than it ought to be. This past year he's been away four times. That's more than ever before."

"It's not like he *wants* to go," Otto said. "He does it for us."

"Maybe." Lucia narrowed her eyes as a new idea formed in her mind. "Or maybe he just says that to make us feel better. I mean, what would *you* rather do: stay in boring, rubbishy Little Tunks or travel to exotic lands?"

"I'd rather stay in Little Tunks," Otto said.

"Well, that's you," she replied, with a dismissive snap of her wrist.

They were silent for another minute, then Lucia spoke in a wilting voice, "I wonder when we'll be sent to Mrs. Carnival."

Above them, Max suddenly tossed violently in his bed, as though the mere mention of Mrs. Carnival had instantaneously brought on a nightmare. He moaned several times and flipped over twice more before he settled down again. Poor Max had it the worst with Mrs. Carnival, you see, because she had an oil cyst on the back of her neck the size of a grape. Every so often she liked it to be squeezed and drained, and Max's fingers, she said, were exactly small and soft enough for the job.

Otto reached up and gently patted Max's leg. As he did, though, his pyjama top lifted and Lucia saw the top of a folded piece of light blue paper sticking out his pyjama bottom's waistband.

"What's that?" she asked.

Otto quickly pulled his top down.

"Nothing," he said.

Lucia studied her brother for a moment. Her heavy black eyebrows lowered and she sucked back her breath in a long hiss. Otto was keeping a secret from her! Never, ever in their entire lives had Otto kept a secret from Lucia! He told her everything, and she him, even the dumbest things. Like when Otto put a dried bean up his nose one morning, just to see, and it came out of his mouth later that afternoon, Lucia was the only one he had told. And just two weeks ago, she had confessed to Otto that she was quite possibly in love with her English teacher, Mr. Dupuis, because he sort of looked like the Sultan of Juwi. Around the chin and eyes.

But now it seemed that Otto had a new secret and he didn't trust Lucia with it. It was intolerable!

She reached out and yanked his pyjama top back up to make a grab for the paper but Otto scooted backwards in his bed before she could get it.

"Show me!" she cried.

"Shh," Otto warned, nodding toward the upper bunk.

"I don't care. I won't have you keeping secrets from me," Lucia said without lowering her voice.

"I'm not," Otto said. "I was just waiting to tell you. Just until I was sure."

"About what?" Lucia said.

"Shh."

Above them, Max groaned and turned.

"Oh, fine," Otto said. From under his pillow he pulled out a torch, and switched it on. Then he pulled the blue paper from his waistband but before he handed it to Lucia, he stared hard at her with a strange expression on his face. It was a look that is commonly used by members of certain tribes in the Amazon, who are about to cross deep gorges via fragile rope bridges. It's a look that says, "Step lightly here, my friend, I beg of you."

Lucia understood the look perfectly, and was thrilled. It meant that something really interesting was about to happen.

"It might be nothing at all, Lucia," Otto said, seeing how his sister's eyes flashed. That always made him nervous. It meant she was getting ideas.

"Yes, yes," Lucia said impatiently, holding her hand out for the paper. "Just show me."

He handed it to her, shining the torch beam on it as she unfolded it.

It was a letter, dated the month before. Here is what it said:

Dear Casper,

Well, I warned you that I was coming to visit one of these days and now I've gone and done it. I even spent my morning "snoring by the sea" until a gull dropped a damn clam on my forehead. I hate the sea. Smells like salty horse manure.

> *I'll see you when I see you.*
> *Your loving aunt-in-law,*
> *Haddie Piggit*

P.S. How much do the kids know about their mother?

P.P.S. If the answer is "Nothing," don't you think it's time you told them?

P.P.P.S. Because if you don't, and they find out, they'll never forgive you. I won't say a word, of course . . . these lips are zipped. This teakettle don't whistle.

Lucia read it over another time, then looked up at Otto.

"Haddie Piggit?" Lucia said. "Who is she? I've never heard of her."

"Well, she signed the letter 'aunt-in-law,' so she must be Mum's aunt," said Otto.

"I know *that!*" Lucia said (she didn't, really). "The point is . . . what do you think the letter *means*?"

"It means that Mum is still alive." This came from

Max, who was now leaning over the edge of the top bunk, looking down at the letter in Lucia's hands.

"Nonsense," Lucia said. "It doesn't say that anywhere. And anyway, I thought you were sleeping."

"At the very least, it means that Dad knows more about what happened to Mum than he's telling us," Max said. "I think we ought to ask him about her again."

"Don't. You know he hates being asked about her," Otto said.

"But she's *our* mother, after all," Max said. "We have a right to know. She'd want us to."

"How do you know that? You barely remember her," Otto said.

Sadly, this was true. Memory, in my opinion, is a complete noodle. It hangs on to the silliest things but forgets the stuff that really matters. The Hardscrabbles had forgotten so much about their mum that she only existed in fragments, like a doll that's been taken apart and has pieces that are lost and others bits that are drawn on with a marker.

Otto, being the oldest, should have remembered her best, but in fact he remembered her least. His memory of her was as vague and ghostly, he told them, as one of Casper's quick charcoal sketches.

Lucia remembered her hands, particularly a constellation of freckles around one of her right knuckles that right side up looked like a bowler hat and upside down looked like a dog with floppy ears. She remembered that same hand running through her own hair, making her feel sweet and drowsy. She remembered having kisses blown at her, and blowing them back, but she couldn't remember the lips that blew them.

It was maddening really.

Max said that the thing he remembered most of all was the way she smelled. He said she smelled of peppermint. When Otto and Lucia told him that of course she did, the whole town smelled of it, he shook his head. "No, it was peppermint that grew from the ground, not the kind that came from the Such Fun Chewing Gum chimneys."

Still, at four o'clock on Tuesdays and Fridays, the Such Fun factory pumped out their mountain mint flavor, which was close, Max said, to Mum's smell. On those days Max liked to sit on the roof and smell the air.

That was all the Hardscrabbles had left of her. No photographs—Casper said she hated to be photographed— few memories, and a father whose face grew so sad when her name was mentioned that they stopped mentioning her at all.

"Think about it logically," Otto said. "If Mum's alive, she knows where to find us. She knows where we live, since we've lived in the same place all our lives. If she's alive and wanted to see us, she might have come whenever she liked. She hasn't, so she doesn't. And if she's dead, well, then what does it all matter?"

They were silent for a moment. Then Lucia said, "So what do we do now?"

"Nothing," Otto said. "Things will go on as just they always have."

Note to reader: If you ever want your life to turn topsy-turvy, say, "Things will go on just as they always—" Oops, I almost said it. Anyway, say the last words that Otto just said. I, however, want to keep my life as normal as possible, so I can get on with writing this book.

Chapter 3

*In which the Hardscrabbles take a train to London,
enter a portal to the Perilous-World-at-Large,
and make a tattooed man really angry*

The following day, when the Hardscrabble children came home from school, they found that their bags were packed and piled near the front door. This was the beginning of things happening that had never happened before.

In the past, they usually had a few weeks between the time Casper started sleeping at night and when he finally sent the children off to stay with Mrs. Carnival. During those weeks, Casper would gently break it to them that he had to go away for a job. He'd show them the place on a map and tell them about the people whom he would be painting, and little by little, the children would ease into the idea of spending time with Mrs. Carnival and her neck cyst.

"What's this?" Otto said to the bags when he and Lucia

walked through the door. Just then, Casper came down the stairs, dressed in regular clothes—black trousers and a mostly clean white button-down shirt.

"Where are you going *this* time?" Lucia asked sullenly.

"It can't be helped," Casper said briskly. "I'm wanted rather suddenly. Prince Andrei's fox has learned to balance a champagne glass on his snout and the prince wants me to paint that into the portrait I've already done, in time for his birthday party. The fox's birthday party, that is. Now, don't look at me that way, Lucia. It won't take more than a few days. You'll all be perfectly fine, but you'll have to hurry. There's a train leaving at four ten. Angela will meet you at the station."

"Angela? You mean your cousin Angela?" Lucia cried, her eyes widening at Otto. "Angela in London?"

"That's right," Casper said. "School is nearly over for the year anyway, so it won't matter that you lose a few days. And Angela hasn't seen you three in ages."

No Mrs. Carnival! *And a few days in London!* Lucia smiled at Otto, and Otto smiled back but not quite as brightly. Leaving Little Tunks always made him nervous.

"Max! *Max?*" Casper called up the stairs. When there was no answer, Casper said, "He must be on the roof. He bolted when I told him. Lucia, go fetch him please. We've only twenty minutes to get out of your school clothes and get to the station."

Lucia ran out the door and round back, where the monstrous oak tree snuggled against the house. Grabbing the lowest branch, she pulled herself up to the first foothold, then carefully began to climb. She was quite a brave person, except when it came to heights. Consequently, the climb was slow and awkward. The worst part was when she reached the roofline. Even though the roof's pitch was not steep, she hated making the small leap off the tree and onto the roof, and feeling that terrifying instant of being unsupported in the air. She might call to Max from the tree, but Max never answered you when you did that. He always made you walk on the main roof and then over on the adjoining roof where the chimney sat.

Lucia made her leap, stifling a gasp of terror as she did so. She landed on the roof, wobbly and breathless. After pausing to collect herself and find her balance, she cautiously made her way towards her brother.

Max was sitting in a lawn chair that was perched precariously across the opening of the chimney. His nose was in the pocket atlas book and he didn't look up, not even when Lucia was right beside him.

"It's no good brooding about it, Max," Lucia said, trying to keep the shakiness out of her voice. "I don't like it either, but we haven't got a choice in the matter. And anyway, it's Angela, not Mrs. Carnival, and it's *London*." She paused, expecting to have to strengthen the argument, or at the worst physically drag Max off the roof, which was far too dangerous for her taste.

"I didn't come up here because of that," Max said, his nose still tucked into the book. Lucia watched him for a minute.

"Was it because of Brenda then?" Lucia asked. "Did the kids at school tell her about Mum?"

Max sighed and looked up. He gazed off into the distance, over the stretch of houses, past the Such Fun factory's chimneys, and to the hills beyond. "I think they must have. She was giving me that look at lunchtime. You know that look?"

Lucia did.

"I'm sorry," Lucia said.

Max shrugged. "Bound to happen, I guess."

That really bothered Lucia. She had always made fun of Max's unfailing optimism about people, but she had also come to count on it.

"Anyway, I'm not up here because of her," he said, standing and dropping the atlas down the chimney. "We'd better go down. We have to catch the four-ten train."

"Then why on earth did you run off like that?" Lucia sniped, angry at having had to make the frightening climb to the roof for nothing.

"Oh, I had some last-minute business to take care of," Max said mysteriously.

No one knew what Max did up on the chimney, and no one cared enough to try to find out. Which just goes to show, you should pay attention to the youngest.

A train ride is nearly always an enjoyable thing. There are views to gaze out upon and sweets to unwrap and people to make fun of. The three Hardscrabble children were very amused by a man sitting across from them who had fallen asleep and was having a conversation with himself.

"Chum, chum, chum, I fancy apples. Better than a kick in the pants, that's for sure, har-har-har!" He was going on like this for some time, and the Hardscrabbles had to squash their hands against their mouths to keep their laughter from waking him up and spoiling their fun. A loud sneeze from the woman behind him startled him awake anyway, and then they had to find something else with which to amuse themselves.

For a while they tried to take an interest in a teenage girl whose eyebrows were pierced and whose hair was dyed green and shaved on the sides.

"You ought to take her photo," Lucia whispered to Otto. (She had urged him to take a camera along to London in case he found curiosities he wanted to capture for his collection.) But by the time he'd gotten the old Nikon camera out of its case, they found that the girl was staring back and seemed equally amused by them, which greatly annoyed the two eldest Hardscrabbles. Lucia puffed out her nostrils and said, "What's wrong with *us*?" while Otto adjusted his scarf and looked away. Max, however, smiled at her. She smiled back and tossed him half of her chocolate bar.

"Are you mad?" Lucia whispered to him as he started to bring it to his mouth. "Don't eat that! It's probably poisoned. Or laced with drugs. Remember Prince Hunai."

Prince Hunai was one of their father's clients who had smoked something strange while making a diplomatic visit with the leader of a nomadic tribe, and had refused to wash his hair ever since. Casper made it look nice in the sketches but he said it smelled like a fish-and-chip shop in mid-August.

Max turned in his seat to face his sister squarely, then stuffed the chocolate in his mouth and smiled at her as he chewed.

"Well, if your lips turn blue and you have a seizure, don't come running to me," Lucia said. She watched Max nervously for a few moments, but his lips only turned chocolaty in the corners. In the end Lucia wished that she'd asked for a bite.

For the rest of the train ride, the children had to make do with their own brains for amusement. Otto slumped back in his seat and pulled his trousers leg up. Extracting a pen from his back pocket, he began to draw a dragon on his knee. Max stared out the window and imagined what it would be like to live in the towns that they passed, where no one had ever heard of the Hardscrabble family.

Lucia opened the book she had brought along. It was a mystery, a type of book that she usually didn't like on account of the fact that bodies were always being found. That reminded her of two things: one, that her mother's body had not been found; and two, that her mother's body might someday be found and she didn't like the thought of that either. Still she had taken this book out of the library because she liked the author's photo on the back, and sometimes that's as good a reason as any.

On page five a body was discovered in a henhouse and it was being pecked apart by the hens. Lucia promptly closed the book but marked her place with a train time-table that had been left on her seat, just in case she found herself in desperate need of reading material on the trip.

She looked out the window and tried to think of poetic things to say about green fields and grazing cows, but the effort made her feel feverish. So instead she thought of the Sultan of Juwi, as usual. I won't tell you *all* of her thoughts about the sultan because they are very personal and none of your business, not to be rude. But I can tell you about the bit in which Lucia imagines seeing the sultan standing by the edge of the Thames. His face is swollen from many beatings by Dr. Azziz and his goon squad. Though he has managed to escape from them, he is suffering from acute amnesia. Probably from all the beatings to the head. In despair, he has decided to pitch himself into the inky depths of the river. Just as he lunges forward toward his death, Lucia grabs his arm and yanks him back to safety.

Right at this moment, a few seats in front of her on the train, Lucia has spied a head that interests her. She can only see the tiniest bit of it above the seat, just a bit of the profile with a delicate nose and a sloping cheekbone, but it's enough for her to imagine that it might be *him*. Let's leave her to her thoughts now.

The Hardscrabbles arrived at St. Pancras station five minutes early (it turned out the sloping-cheekboned head belonged to a middle-aged woman!), so it was no cause for panic when they found that Angela was not at the station. She was a very rush-about sort of person, always arriving late and breathless. They stood around for a good ten minutes, watching all the people bustling across the platform. So many gloriously unfamiliar faces! A few people glanced at the Hardscrabbles longer than usual, noting that they were a good-looking trio, but otherwise the children were deliciously anonymous. It was like a vacation from being Hardscrabbles.

After twenty minutes, they all sat down on their bags, and after twenty-five minutes their chins were anxiously digging into their palms.

"Do you think she's forgotten?" Max asked.

"How could she forget? Dad just talked to her today," Lucia said.

"Maybe Dr. Jekyll got sick," Otto said. "And she had to rush him to the veterinarian's."

"Maybe they'll give him a lobotomy while he's there," Max said. He hated that dog and the feeling was mutual.

"Anyway, I think I remember the way to her flat. Sort of," Lucia said. "We might as well just meet her there. What do you say?"

Max thought yes, but Otto said no and persuaded them to wait another ten minutes. But when Angela still didn't appear he had to give in to their plan.

They examined a tube map hanging on the wall and, mostly through Max's excellent sense of direction, they managed to make their way to Camden Town. There was the moment of triumph when they found themselves on Fishtail Lane, Angela's cramped side street. The sooty brick houses were pressed together, shoulder to shoulder, and

Angela's building was the narrowest of them all. As they entered the building, the Hardscrabbles felt the thrill of a quest successfully completed and the budding sense that their street savvy was equal to any native Londoner's. They also felt more kindly towards Angela. Back when they had been fumbling through the tube station, their bags pummeling their thighs, they were saying things like "Angela is such a featherbrain!" "She'd forget her own ears if they weren't fastened to her head." But now they were saying, "Won't Angela be amazed that we found her place so easily!" "I can't wait to see her again, silly old thing!"

They walked up the three flights of stairs and Lucia rapped on Angela's door. Instantly, they heard Dr. Jekyll explode with frenzied barking.

"It's okay, Dr. Jekyll! It's only us!" Max yelled back at him. That only made the barking more furious.

"He hates you the most, you know," Otto said.

They waited for the sound of Angela's footsteps, but the only thing they heard was Dr. Jekyll's toenails clicking against the floor as he paced in front of the door. They knocked again, sending the dog into a new fit of rage. But still no Angela.

"Well, this rots," said Lucia.

"Maybe she's waiting for us at St. Pancras," Max suggested. "Maybe we've crisscrossed."

"We're not going back there," Otto declared. He'd been a good sport about traipsing through London thus far, but he'd had enough of adventure for the day. "We'll just stay put and wait."

He dropped his bag down and sat on it. Lucia and Max, seeing that he would not be budged, relented and did the same. There they waited, in the dingy little hallway, listening to Dr. Jekyll's pacing and nodding a sheepish hello to a red-faced man who passed them on his way upstairs. They nodded hello again when he went back down the stairs a while later, then again when he came back up with a bag of groceries.

"Who are you wanting, then?" he demanded in the tone of someone who had had enough monkey business.

"Well, seeing as how we've been sitting in front of Angela Winger's door for the past half hour, I'd say it's a safe bet we're wanting Angela Winger," Lucia said without even looking at him. She was sometimes rude to people who asked dumb things.

"Angela's on holiday," the man spat back. "Piss off!" He jabbed his thumb at the stairs.

"What do you mean she's on holiday?" Lucia said, looking up at the man.

"Oh, the little snit is interested now, is she?" The man smirked and cocked his head in a taunting way.

"Excuse me, sir"—Max tried to be as polite as possible to make up for Lucia—"but where *is* Angela?"

"Not that it's any of your business," he said, "but she happens to be in Berlin. As in Germany."

"But our dad talked to her today and she said she'd meet us at the station," Lucia said.

"And *did* she meet you at the station?" the man asked in a mocking tone.

"No," Lucia admitted. "But . . . but she can't be in Berlin!"

"Can be and is, Sunshine. Can be and is." The man was enjoying himself so much now that he put his bag of groceries on the floor and seemed prepared to stay and watch the panic unfold.

It did.

"What do we do now?"

"How could Dad have sent us if Angela's away?"

But Max had the wherewithal to ask the man, "What about Dr. Jekyll then? She wouldn't just leave him behind."

"Ever heard of a dog walker? She was here this afternoon. Dr. Jekyll would have took her fingers off for her if I hadn't gone in first and gave him what for. And did that sullen little minger even say thanks for my trouble?" He frowned remembering this snub afresh. "Now, clear out! The building don't allow loitering in the hallways."

There was nothing to do but to gather up their bags once more and trudge back down the stairs and out onto the street.

"What are we supposed to do now?" Otto said. They were silent for a bit, considering.

"I might try climbing up," Max suggested, eyeing the gate in front of the building and the tiers of balconies above. "I could try Angela's window and see if I can get in that way."

"Yes, and then we'll all spend a lovely night in jail. Brilliant, Max," Lucia said.

In truth, she was slightly jealous of the idea, because

though it involved risk and danger, of which she very much approved, it also involved heights, which as you already know she is not fond of.

"What we need to do is to ring Dad," Otto said. This was so plainly obvious that no one could argue against it. They found a phone booth on the next block and Max dialed up their home number. He held the phone to his ear for a distressingly long time before he hung up.

"He must have already left," he said.

They had no other phone number for him. When he went away on his trips, he always called *them* and gave Mrs. Carnival a number in case of emergencies.

"Maybe that man in Angela's building was wrong," Max said. "Or maybe he was just having us on, and Angela will be back later."

There was hope in that thought and they didn't have much else at the moment. Otto was for planting themselves outside Angela's building and waiting for her to return. But Lucia argued that since they were in the middle of London and free to do what they liked, they might as well try to have an adventure. Max agreed and so that was that.

It wasn't long, though, before Otto began to think it was a good idea as well. The whole of Camden was crawling with oddities, and there was nothing that Otto liked better than an oddity. People with pink hair, blue hair, black lipstick (on men!), ears that were stretched wide with huge disk earrings, and every available patch of skin pierced or tattooed. The children stared at them in much the same way that people in Little Tunks stared at the

Hardscrabbles—with a mixture of curiosity and uneasiness.

"Do you think they're dangerous?" Otto asked, which ironically is something people often asked about him.

"Very, I'm sure," Lucia said. It was a waste of everyone's time to have an adventure without the element of danger.

"Rubbish," Max said. "Anyone can put on clumpy black boots and pierce themselves silly. A truly dangerous person would be someone you'd never even look at twice."

They wandered through the outdoor markets, a jungle of circus-coloured clothing and shoes and wild wigs and everything else you could imagine. They saw boots that had plastic heels with tiny plastic goldfish swimming in them, necklaces made out of old typewriter keys, and shirts made out of mice bones. The children were so fascinated that they forgot to mind about lugging their bags around. They even nearly forgot their messy predicament. They ambled through the streets, gazing into shop windows, their healthy pink Little Tunks lungs eagerly pulling in the stink of coach fumes and Indian curry and occasionally some really impressive body odor.

Then suddenly, without realizing it, they found a secret opening into the Perilous-World-at-Large. There are lots of these openings scattered about at certain longitudes and latitudes. There is one, for instance, right outside El Djem, Tunisia, and another to the left of a raspberry bush on Mr. DiMorelli's dairy farm in Stone Mills, New York. Most people pass through one or two at some point in their lives without realizing it. But if they were paying attention they'd notice that far more perilous things begin to happen to them almost immediately. The Hardscrabbles certainly had no idea that anything unusual had occurred when they entered the portal on Camden High Street although Lucia swears that she felt dizzy, but Max says that was due to the coach fumes.

Otto stopped short quite suddenly.

He was staring at a man perched on a parked car. The man's head was shaved and he wore no shirt. Every inch of exposed skin was tattooed, even his scalp and face, which had fierce-looking swirls covering it. His lips were blue. It took a moment to see that the blue was not lipstick, but a tattoo that stained his lips and covered his chin. It looked as though he'd eaten blue ice cream and it had dribbled down his chin in curling rivulets.

"And I suppose *he's* not dangerous either?" Lucia said to Max.

Max didn't answer. He was looking at the man thoughtfully. Actually he was looking at the man with a stupid expression on his face, but he always looked stupid when he was doing his best thinking. The man was obviously used to being looked at and he ignored them.

"There's one for your collection." Lucia nudged her elbow into Otto's side.

That's all she said. It was completely innocent, but of course they all blamed her later for what happened.

Otto whipped his camera off his shoulder and began to fumble with the case, and then with the lens cap.

"I wonder," Max said, the stupid expression now gone

from his face, "if that man knows he's wearing a woman's tattoo on his face?"

"What do you mean?" Lucia asked.

"Well, the Maori people in New Zealand tattoo their faces just like that, only the men have one sort of tattoo and the women have another. That bloke has a lady's tattoo on his face."

Otto snapped a picture. The tattooed man's head swiveled sharply at the sound of the click. Lady tattoo or not, the sight of that face staring directly at them made their eyes go wide. His nose had the oddest shape. It looked like a frog that had been smashed flat in the road. Maybe he'd tattooed his face to take people's attention off the smashed frog in the center of it.

"That'll be a fiver," the man said, hopping off the car and heading toward them while holding out his palm.

"Five pounds? What on earth for?" Lucia said. Her brothers were simply staring with their mouths open.

"Well, I ain't a bloody penguin in a zoo," he replied as though he were genuinely offended. "Tourists pay five pounds for my picture."

"Ridiculous," Lucia said firmly, and she grabbed Otto and Max by the shirtsleeves and stalked off, not paying any attention as the man yelled after them, "Oi, oi!"

Lucia's impressive eyebrows squinched together. "That's nerve to make people pay for his photo."

Secretly, though, she was not so much offended by the five pounds as by the fact that he had called them tourists.

"Anyway," she said, "it's about time we had some dinner. I'm starving."

Otto suggested trying back at Angela's again, just in case her neighbour was wrong and Angela had returned, but Lucia refused. She said it would be a shame to leave the streets of Camden just yet, now that they could do whatever they damn well pleased. Max agreed and Otto did too in the end. All in all they were in that gorgeous state of mind in which they felt free and unafraid and sharply aware of how large and exciting the world was.

In other words, it hadn't gotten dark outside yet.

Chapter 4

In which Lucia reveals a secret
and the Princess Uzima narrowly
escapes from a lion

Casper always gave them some spending money when he went away, and now they considered what sort of dinner they should buy with it. There were so many choices here! In Little Tunks there was only a tiny fish-and-chip shop, a pizza parlour, and the Pig & Pony Pub, where they served a dried-out disk of brown substance that the menu called a burger.

The Hardscrabbles peered through the windows at a good many food shops and were tempted by some. But they couldn't all agree on a place until they passed the open door of a curry shop and smelled the earthy tangle of spices, so strong that the odor oozed down the back of their throats and made them feel all spitty. In a good way. They went in and ordered at the counter, each choosing something different so that they could try a bit of everything. They sat at a table by the window, so as not to miss a thing on the street. After several minutes, the shop owner brought them their food, along with small silver pots of gem-colored sauces.

"Careful," he warned, pointing to a pot of red sauce. "This one is veerry, veerry spicy."

So of course the red sauce was the first pot that the Hardscrabbles dipped their spoons in. After a few minutes, their noses were dripping and they were making some strange *chockety* sounds in their throats until the shop owner brought over some yoghurt to cool them down. After they were done, Otto wanted to leave for Angela's but Lucia insisted that they sit and digest. This should have struck her brothers as strange, since she'd never cared about their digestion in the past, but they didn't notice. They all sat and digested until the shop owner started to give them filthy looks.

With their bellies full and their heads feeling strangely light, they walked back to Fishtail Lane and climbed the steps to Angela's flat. Their rap on the door provoked the usual fit of barking from Dr. Jekyll, but this time they also heard the approach of footsteps on the other side of the door.

"There, you see!" Max said, smiling. "She *is* here after all."

But when the door opened, it wasn't Angela at all. It was a stocky teenage girl with a wide, flat face and a badly chapped lower lip. Dr. Jekyll ran between her legs and flew out into the hall, barking wildly.

"He bites," she shouted in order to be heard above the barking.

"It's okay, boy," Max said to Dr. Jekyll. "It's just us." He put his hand out and the dog lunged forward and snapped, grazing Max's fingers.

"I told you," the girl said flatly.

"Are you the dog walker?" Lucia asked.

"S'right." The girl eyed Lucia suspiciously. "Who are you?"

"We're the Hardscrabbles. We're supposed to be staying with Angela for a few days."

"How you going to do that when she's in Germany?"

"Then it's true!" Otto exclaimed.

"What's he doing with his hands?" The girl scowled suspiciously at Otto.

"Just talking. But look," Lucia said, "there must be some mistake. Our dad called Angela today and arranged it all."

The girl opened her mouth, then shut it again. She grew very red in the face.

"Well, how was I supposed to understand what he was saying with all the barking and whatnot," she muttered crossly.

"You spoke to our dad?" Max asked.

"I might have." The girl frowned and picked at a loose bit of skin on her lower lip. "I don't know. *Some*one called. And they said *some*thing about a favor and then about St. Pancras, but here was Dr. Jekyll going berserk like he does, and I just said 'Yeh, sure,' like that. Just to get him off the phone. How was I supposed to know—"

This girl was obviously such a twit that the Hard-scrabbles blotted her out, the way you might stick your thumb over the face of a person in a photo whom you can't stand.

"Look," Lucia said to her brothers, "we might stay anyway. We'd have the place all to ourselves. Imagine living in London, completely on our own?"

"I don't like it," Otto said.

"It's better than Mrs. Carnival's," Max said.

"What? Do you think I'm some sort of duffer?" the dog walker cried, forcing them to remember that she existed. "How do I know you aren't just a pack of thieves?"

"You just said you spoke to our dad," Lucia said.

"I said *maybe* I did. You lot got a shifty look. Especially him." She pointed to Otto. "No, you can't stay here. I won't be blamed for her stuff going missing." She reached down, grabbed Dr. Jekyll by his collar, and yanked him back in the flat. "You'll just have to go straight back to where you came from." Then she shut the door in their faces.

They stood there in silence for a moment.

"Mrs. Carnival's cyst has probably filled back up since the last time I drained it," Max said dolefully.

"So much for not having to finish out the school year," Otto griped. "Mrs. Carnival will make us go."

"So much for London," said Max.

"Not quite," Lucia said. "We'll be in London for twelve more hours yet."

Now we come to the part where Lucia divulges a secret. She's known it since the train ride and she told it to the readers in the first draft of this book, but when she read it over she decided it was better to keep it to herself until this moment. The element of surprise and all that.

"The last train for Little Tunks has left at seven thirty," she said. "There won't be another one till seven forty-five tomorrow morning." She said this very stiffly, because it had that significant sort of feel to it. Also, she was slightly nervous about how her brothers would react.

She is happy to say they were fairly good sports. Except that Otto said, "Where in the world do you expect us to sleep?" and Max said, "That was really stupid." But she suspects Max was simply upset because for once she knew something that he didn't (if you remember, she had used the train timetable as a bookmark, and she happened to notice the time of the last train and the first train to Little Tunks).

"Look," Lucia said in a very reasonable tone, "when do the *really* interesting things happen? Not when you've brushed your teeth and put on your pyjamas and are cozy in bed. They happen when you are cold and uncomfortable and hungry and don't have a roof over your head for the night."

"Who told you *that*?" Otto said, scowling.

"It's just common sense, isn't it?" Lucia replied.

"The Princess Uzima said it," Max put in. "*After* her mother-in-law kicked her out of the palace with nothing but the clothes on her back."

There was a pastel sketch of the Princess Uzima in their hallway. It showed an elegant, slender woman with

58

skin the color of polished cherrywood and the most disdainful nostrils that Lucia had ever seen. She had married the tribal prince of Anawadi but her mother-in-law thought she was too stuck-up. She had the princess arrested for treason and tossed out into the wilderness, leaving her with nothing but a vial of poison so that she could kill herself before the lions did it for her. But Princess Uzima was not afraid of lions. She struggled across the plains of Africa, sleeping under trees, sipping bitter water from the okanobu plant, and once even escaping from a lion by throwing back her head and baring her elegant throat, then daring him to bite it. When he hesitated, she cursed him in the Anawadi tongue and threw stones at him until he ran off. In Casper's sketch, you could see a tiny silver vial hanging from a chain around the princess's neck. It still held the poison that she had refused to swallow.

"Yes, and the point is things *did* get really interesting for her then," Lucia said.

Otto looked unconvinced but Max said, "In any case, it's twelve hours less of Mrs. Carnival and her neck cyst. Well done on that count, Lucia."

Chapter 5

In which London grows dark

There is nothing like a darkening sky to knock the wind out of a *really* interesting experience. And the London sky was growing very dark very quickly. For the first time that day, the Hardscrabbles were beginning to understand the seriousness of their situation. They were all alone with not much money and nowhere to go. In the daylight, the streets of Camden were colorful and exotic. Yes, some of the people had looked a bit scary, but none of the Hardscrabbles had truly felt like they were in any danger. Not really and truly.

Now, as they made their way back down Fishtail Lane and toward the market area, they gazed around apprehensively. The market stalls were closed and the streets were more empty. Or rather, they were more full of the wrong sort of people. The dimming light sopped up the bright pinks of wigs and the chartreuse greens of stockings and now everyone looked grey and grim. People moved more slowly too and seemed to notice each other more. The Hardscrabbles felt eyes on them; curious, interested eyes.

They wandered aimlessly until Max stopped and dropped his bag on the ground. "We can't just walk around all night," he said. "And anyway, my arms are ready to fall off from carrying this bag."

"We might try and find a police officer," Otto suggested.

"Don't be silly. The police don't bother themselves about little things like this," Lucia said. "We'll just have to find some place to tuck ourselves away for the night. An alley, maybe."

Otto made a face. "Bad things happen in alleys."

"That's just in books," Lucia said. "By the way, what's that smell?"

They all smelled the smell then. It had been there the whole time they were talking, of course, but they hadn't noticed it. It was a green fishy smell. Not a "green fish" smell. I mean green in the sense that it smelled alive. Also it smelled of fish.

Max walked up to the low fence that lined the street and leaned over.

"It's the canal," he said.

Indeed, right below them was a long canal and drifting slowly through the water was a narrow boat, the lights from its windows skimming the quiet banks.

"Let's find a place down there," Lucia said brightly. "You never read about murders by the edge of a canal."

Of course bodies are always being found floating in canals in mystery books, but as you know, Lucia rarely read mystery books so she couldn't have known that.

They walked down a set of stairs and passed across a bridge on which several rough-looking people were draped against the railing. The Hardscrabbles pretended not to notice them. They fervently hoped that the people on the bridge would do the same.

"Well hello, kiddies." The girl was maybe seventeen. A cigarette dangled from her lips and she was dead thin. So thin, in fact, it was amazing she could hold herself upright, since there was a mass of thick blond dreadlocks spilling out of her skull. She looked a bit like a willow tree.

"Running away from home, are we?" she asked.

"Not at all," Max replied. "It's just that we've missed the last train home and we're looking for a place to sleep for the night."

"Don't talk to her!" Lucia hissed. "Honestly, Max, you are *just* the type who winds up dead in an alley."

"Come on with me then," the girl said, flicking her cigarette into the water. "I know a canal boat that's empty, up the way a bit. Good for squatting."

"That would be great—" Max started to say, but Lucia cut him off.

"We're perfectly fine as is," she said brusquely. Then she remembered that willows were her favorite tree and they so often toppled pathetically during bad winds, so she added, "But thank you. Good night."

"What about the pretty blond boy?" the girl said,

nodding toward Otto. "He's quite dishy. Want to come home with me, love?"

That made Lucia want to slap her, willow tree or not. Otto's one visible eye went wide and his head dipped so low that it nearly disappeared inside his scarf.

They walked away quickly and didn't say a word to one another for a while. I think it was because they were embarrassed.

Spare boxes and places to sleep for the night, same thing—there aren't as many of them as you'd think. They searched and searched for an out-of-the-way nook, and when they finally found one, it was so narrow that they would have had to sleep standing up, shoulder to shoulder, and they did have enough sense to know that they'd want to kill each other after ten minutes like that.

"Where did the Princess Uzima sleep?" Otto asked.

They all thought a minute, trying to remember what Casper had told them.

"She slept in a car for a while, I remember," Lucia said.

"That was later. The first few nights she slept under a baobab tree," Max said.

And there, just ahead of them, was a tremendous tree by the edge of the canal where there had been very few trees along the way and small ones at that. No one even bothered to say "That's weird" because it so clearly was. It also smacked of the supernatural, which none of them believed in, so they decided to pretend it was exactly what they had expected would happen. Lucia even hesitated about sleeping there, because it was a willow tree and therefore reminded her of the horrible dreadlocked thing on the bridge. But in the end she realized that she'd loved willows long before she hated the girl on the bridge so it was probably okay.

They pushed through the fountain of delicate branches, the leaves lisping as they parted, and they found a nice circle of clean bare earth inside. It was so well sheltered that even the smell of the canal was fainter and all the sounds from outside were muffled. They dropped their bags, and then themselves, to the ground. For some time, they sat in silence, listening to the smothered voices of passersby and the very faint nighttime hum of the city. They were small-town people, after all, and at the end of a day full of crowds and noise they were grateful to be alone again. A streetlight on the canal path not far from the tree shed a milky yellow light that leaked between the leaves and gave them enough illumination to see by. With some squinting Lucia might have read a book or Otto might have tattooed himself. It was the perfect little hut.

"Hey, you know what?" Max said. "We could stay right here instead of going back to Little Tunks. We'd have to be careful with money, of course, but this tree is nearly as good as a tent and we've always wanted to go camping."

It was a really excellent idea and they all agreed, even Otto.

"Good, that's settled," Lucia said. "Now I think we should all brush our teeth because our breaths stink like an open sewer, what with the curry and all."

There was a small argument then. I won't write it out

because it was too stupid, but it was about something Lucia had said earlier regarding teeth brushing and which Max had taken very literally, which was typical of him.

In the end they dug through their bags and pulled out their toothbrushes. The toothpaste was in Max's bag. It was a very dry brushing. They parted the willow branches and spit outside the tree so things didn't get repulsive inside.

Max put his toothbrush and paste back in his bag then began to rummage through his clothes. He frowned and searched around the bag some more.

"Spoon's not here." He looked up at them with an alarmed expression on his face.

"It must be, look again," Lucia said.

Max did and Otto scooted over next to him to look as well. After a few moments, Otto looked up at Lucia and shook his head.

"Well, Dad must have forgotten, that's all," she said. "He was in a hurry."

"He's never forgotten before," said Max. He looked genuinely stricken.

Spoon is a spoon. He's made of sheeny silver-colored material and is stuffed with batting and has a sly, smiling face embroidered on. Max has slept with him since he was an infant. You might think it's immature for a ten-year-old to still sleep with a stuffed toy but Spoon has what you might call Special Family Meaning. Spoon was part of a set that was given to Otto when he was a baby (though no one remembers who gave it to him). The set was based on the nursery rhyme "Hey Diddle Diddle the Cat and the Fiddle." When it was new it had seven stuffed pieces—Cat, Fiddle, Cow, Moon, Dog, Dish, and Spoon. Otto lost Fiddle and played with Cat so much that it became too thin-skinned to hold its stuffing, and was thrown out. Moon was set on fire in an experiment, but Otto would rather we not go into that. When the set was handed down to Lucia, she managed to stuff Cow down the toilet within the first week but she held on to Dish and Dog for many years until she left them out in the garden overnight and Dish and Dog were carried off by something. So by the time the set came into Max's possession there was only Spoon left and, curiously, the box that held the set, which says on the back that the nursery rhyme was based on something that happened in the court of Queen Elizabeth I in which her serving girl (Dish) fell in love with the royal food taster (Spoon) and they eloped. But they were caught and were locked in the Tower of London. I think it's very twisted of people to sneak these things into kids' mouths through nursery rhymes, incidentally. But that's another issue altogether.

The week that Mum went missing, Spoon went missing too. When Max couldn't find Spoon, he carried on like a maniac, kicking the wall and sobbing on the floor, and none of the Hardscrabbles knew what to do. I think it was because they all felt like carrying on like that on account of Mum, but instead they were all very quiet because Dad was. They needed something to do, though, so they went on a massive search for Spoon, scouring every cranny of the house and the garden. It took their minds off Mum, and when they found Spoon crammed between the oven and the wall, it made them all feel that everything would be okay. That they would find Mum too, eventually.

So you can see why Spoon held Special Family Meaning, and why Max slept with it every single night, and why it was such a big deal when Dad forgot to pack it. It gave them all an eerie feeling that something was wrong.

Otto said, "Do you think Dad has ditched us?"

In each of their bellies, they felt a swelling of fear, like a balloon that was slowly being filled with *pooshy* breaths. Spoon had not been packed . . . *poosh* . . . the fact that Angela was not home . . . *poosh* . . . and wouldn't Dad find it far more preferable to live in an exotic location than in dull old Little Tunks . . . *poosh, poosh, poosh* . . . and then—most horrible of all—maybe the police's initial suspicions about Dad were true. Maybe he is a psycho who murdered Mum and now he's abandoned his children. They stared at one another with quiet dread in their eyes.

Lucia was the first to let some of the air out of the balloons. "Dad would never just abandon us," she said, her dark brows knitted.

"No. Of course he wouldn't," Max agreed.

Otto still looked grim, but he said, "When we see him, he'll have something to answer for about this whole business."

The other two quickly took up his righteous anger: "If

he hadn't been in such a hurry to leave, he would have realized that it wasn't Angela on the phone," and "Wait until he hears what we've been through—he'll feel awful."

The balloons in their bellies gradually deflated and they began to feel the exhaustion of a most unusual day.

"You can't imagine how badly I have to pee," Max said.

"Not in here," Lucia warned.

"Where then?"

"Pee in the canal," Lucia said.

"That's polluting," Max said.

"Well, fish do," Lucia said.

This argument went on for a few minutes.

"He can pee just outside the tree, if no one's looking," Otto said, sick of the argument. "I've got to go too."

And so did Lucia, now that she thought about it. They stepped through the fountain of branches and waited until they were sure the coast was clear. Max and Otto went right away but Lucia just couldn't do it. It wasn't that she was fussy; it's only that there are some things you just can't force.

"I'll need a restroom," she said firmly.

"Ha! And where do you suppose the Princess Uzima found a restroom on the African plains?" Max said.

"Well, if there were nothing but scrub and gazelles in London, I'd pee in public as well," she snapped back.

"You're just being difficult," Max said.

"Oh? What's that then? A gazelle?" Lucia cried. It was pure luck that a man with a goatee had suddenly appeared on the canal path, heading their way.

"Well, where do you propose that we find a restroom?" Max asked.

"Ever heard of a pub, genius?" Lucià said.

Suddenly she felt her heart beating faster for no reason, so she knew that Otto was scared.

She looked at him and found that he was staring fixedly at the approaching man. She glanced at the man again. She didn't like the way he was walking. It was too fast and too purposeful for a lonely promenade at night.

A shaft of lamplight lit his face briefly, but it was long enough for Lucia to see that she had been mistaken about the goatee. He didn't have one. It was the swirling tattoos on his chin that had given that impression.

"Let's go!" Lucia hissed.

"Oh, for goodness' sakes, Lucia. Just wait till the man passes and *then* go pee," Max said. "Tell her she's being a git, Otto."

But Otto was also staring at the tattooed man, who was now fast approaching. Max turned to look at the man too.

"Isn't that—?" Max started.

The man started running towards them now.

"Move, Otto!" Lucia commanded.

"Stay right there, you filthy—" The tattooed man then said some really awful stuff that I won't repeat. The Hardscrabbles were all so shocked that they didn't move, which was the worst thing they could have done. The man barreled into Otto, lowering his head and smashing it so hard against Otto's chest that Otto flew backwards, right through the branches of the willow and into their make-shift hut. The man burst in after him and shoved Otto up against the tree trunk in the most brutal way.

"Leave him alone!" Lucia screamed as she and Max rushed up behind the man. She was too surprised for tears. There was only the punching of her heart in her chest.

"You owe me twenty quid," the man spat at Otto.

"Twenty? But you said it was five," Max protested.

The man smiled at Otto in a horrible way, his flattened frog's nose pressing even flatter against his face. "Penalty for nicking."

"Give him the money, Otto," Lucia said, her voice shamefully high-pitched.

Otto hesitated and the man grabbed Otto by the throat. Well, he meant to, anyway, but he really grabbed him by the scarf.

"Come on, you little (again, unmentionable), pay up before I start stomping on your ribs." Then Frog Nose yanked the scarf so roughly that it unlooped around Otto's neck and slid right off, falling to the ground.

That was when Lucia knew something bad was about to happen. No one had ever touched his scarf. Even the teachers in school never insisted that he remove it, though outerwear like hats and gloves and scarves was forbidden in the classroom. They knew instinctively that this silent, strange boy would not tolerate it, that he needed the scarf more than they needed him to remove it.

Now Otto's head jerked up. Beneath his long fringe of hair, his one visible eye was wild with rage. In a flash, he grabbed the camera off the branch on which he'd hung it, and with a single, powerful swing, he whipped it against the side of Frog Nose's face. It made a crunching noise, but whether it was the shattering of the camera's inner workings or of bones, it was hard to say. Frog Nose yelped, doubled over, and clutched at his face.

"Run, run!" Lucia cried, but Otto wouldn't. He was in a frenzy and it was doubtful that he could hear anything at all except for the blood rushing through his ears. He swung the camera over his left shoulder and struck again, this time hitting the back of Frog Nose's head. The man stumbled and fell to the ground, howling, but still Otto wouldn't stop. He was getting ready to attack again when Max leapt forward and grabbed the camera right before the next swing.

"I'll kill you!" Frog Nose roared, his voice strangely muffled sounding. Blood was streaming from his nose and from a gash on his temple, and it was dripping into his mouth and down the front of his shirt. At the sight of it, Lucia sucked back her breath. She felt a confusing tangle of emotions—shock at Otto's ferocity. Admiration even. And terror for what had been unleashed.

It also made her think about the rumors back in Little Tunks, about how Otto had strangled their mum in a fit of rage.

Stop thinking about that! she told herself sternly. *It's nonsense! If you want to think about something, think about a way to get us out of this awful mess!*

And that's exactly what she did. Scooping up Otto's

scarf from the ground, she screamed at him, "Run! Run now or I'll throw your scarf in the canal!"

It worked. Otto ran. They all three of them legged it down the canal path and through the streets of Camden Town, and they didn't stop until they found themselves directly in front of the train station.

Chapter 6

In which the Hardscrabbles meet a Viking,
a zebra, and a bogus wild boar.
Also there's a cat.

It was very unfortunate that they had left their bags under the willow tree, but there was nothing to be done about it. They couldn't go back and fetch them—Frog Nose might be waiting for them there.

"Good thing Spoon wasn't in the bag, eh?" Max said, trying to see the bright side.

"Yes, but our return tickets to Little Tunks were," Lucia reminded him.

"I have enough money to buy us all new tickets," Otto said, checking his pocket, "but that will leave us with almost nothing. And where are we supposed to spend the night until the train comes?"

"I've been thinking of something," Max said. "I thought of it before, actually, but I figured we'd first try Lucia's plan of sleeping in London. And since that was clearly a failure—"

"Through no fault of my own!" Lucia reminded him.

"I was thinking," Max continued, "that we might go to Great-aunt Haddie's."

"Who?" Lucia asked.

"*Great-aunt Haddie,*" Max repeated. "She wrote the letter to Dad."

"Oh, yes, I didn't hear what you said," Lucia said, embarrassed that she didn't remember the name or even realize that their mum's aunt would be their great-aunt. "Stellar idea except for the fact that we have no clue where she lives."

"Yes, we do," Max said. "It said so in the letter."

"No, it didn't," Lucia said.

"Yes, it did," Max insisted. "Think about it. She wrote that she'd spent the morning snoring by the sea, in quotation marks. Well, that was her being clever. I checked the pocket atlas and there it was. Snoring-by-the-Sea."

"Is that what you were doing up on the roof?" Lucia asked.

Max nodded.

"You could have just read it in your bedroom and spared me the climb," Lucia said.

"Anyway," Max said, "Snoring-by-the-Sea is a small town and I'll bet there aren't many Haddie Piggits living there. We could just turn up and ask how to find her. Also, it's not too far from London so there still might be some late trains running."

"Snoring-by-the-Sea?" Lucia said, wrinkling her nose. "It doesn't sound very exciting."

"It's better than Mrs. Carnival's," Max said.

It so happened that there *was* a late train and they just managed to catch it. A train ride is nearly always an enjoyable thing, except when it's the second one of the day and you are going to see a relative whom you know nothing about. Also, it's not much fun when it's dark outside. There was little to see through the windows. Here and there they could make out shadowy hummocks of fields or a blocky cluster of houses. There was something very humiliating about this trip too. Lucia, for one, felt as though she had botched things up. Maybe she should have tried harder to keep the adventure going. Who knew when they would ever get to be on their own in London again? Never probably.

"I don't expect Haddie Piggit will be happy to see us," Otto said miserably. "Not at this time of night."

"Of course she'll be happy to see us," Max said. "She's our aunt, isn't she?"

"Great-aunt," Otto said. "Which means she's ancient and probably goes to bed at eight o'clock. After she's eaten her mushy peas."

Presently, Snoring-by-the-Sea was announced as the next stop. The Hardscrabbles grabbed for their bags, then remembered that they didn't have them anymore. It's a very discombobulating feeling to walk off a train at a strange station without having a bag to hold.

Under the flickering platform lamps they could see

that the station was completely deserted. Not a single passenger had gotten off the train and not a single person was waiting to get on. It was altogether ominous, rather like in those old-time books in which the children arrive at a bleak little town and are driven by a creepy coachman to the creepy house of a deeply creepy relative. Even Max glanced back at the train, as though he were wondering if it was too late to get back on. But the next moment the train's horn blew a wheezy warning and it started up again. Then it was gone. The Hardscrabbles were completely and utterly alone.

"Now what?" Lucia turned on Max very snappishly.

"Now we find someone to ask about Haddie Piggit," Max said, trying to sound more confident than he was.

For a solid thirty seconds Otto and Lucia stared at Max. A solid thirty seconds is a long time to stare at someone. Try it and you'll notice that the other person will pretend to be fascinated by a smooshed piece of gum on the pavement. That's exactly what Max was doing at that moment.

"And where, do you suggest, are we going to find this person to ask?" Lucia finally demanded.

Max didn't answer. He just started walking. There was nothing for Otto and Lucia to do but follow him. One, because they were not so coldhearted as to let their youngest sibling wander around a strange place by himself, and two, because they didn't want to be left alone to wander around a strange place without their youngest sibling. Max always seemed to know so much more about real-life things than they did, like how to get from one place to another.

Still, they did mutter to each other as they walked along (Otto often had to repeat himself since it was hard for Lucia to see his hands in the darkness):

"This is taking things pretty far, I'd say," said Otto, gazing at the black stretch of fields all around them. "Sometimes I think Max is quite mental."

"It's just that Dad always indulges him. Because he's the youngest, of course. He ought to be more strict with him. I think I'll have a chat with Dad when he gets back."

And the two continued this "older brother-and-sister conversation" because it made them feel a little less nervous about travelling to who-knew-where in the middle of the night.

Soon a lone farmhouse appeared, with a tumbledown barn behind it. A low groaning sound made Otto and Lucia stop short and stare at each other, their eyes wide.

"Cows," Max called back, without turning or slowing his pace.

Lucia forced her nostrils to flare but it was too dark for anyone to notice. Otto yanked on the end of his scarf so that it was wrapped tight around his neck, and they continued on.

More and more houses began to appear until they came to the heart of a small town. It looked so similar to Little Tunks—the small tidy shops, now closed of course, and the rows of brick houses with their scrappy little front yards—that it made Otto and Lucia relax a bit. They even began to peer at the shop windows, most of which were too dark to see into. But there was one towards the edge of the town, where the shops began to dwindle, that had a single light on towards the back, enough to illuminate a front window and the sign above it—SAINT GEORGE'S TAXIDERMY & CURIOSITIES. The window display had a spooky-looking collection: stuffed rabbits frozen in mid-hop, stuffed foxes frozen in mid-leap, and a miniature zebra that looked out quizzically at them with glinting black eyes. There were several cylindrical-shaped glass contain-ers that imprisoned stuffed ducks and owls, and various horns were scattered all about. The centerpiece, however, was a wild boar. The beast was standing with its huge snout pointing upwards. Its mouth was open in a snarl, baring its white curving tusks. Someone had painted the tips of the lower tusks bright red as though it had recently gored someone.

"It's hideous," Lucia said quietly, unable to tear her eyes away from the beast's face.

"It's fake," Max said. "That's just a very large pig with tusks stuck into its jaws."

"How do you know?" Lucia asked.

"For one thing, only male wild boars have tusks. That one is a girl."

"Really?"

Lucia and Otto both ducked their heads and tipped them to one side to have a better look.

"You're right," Lucia said, then suddenly cried, "Oh!" and drew back.

"What?" Otto asked.

"There. Look on the floor, right by the boar's hind legs," she said.

"Pig," Max corrected, but he crouched down along with Otto and they saw a stuffed black cat, curled in a sleek ball on the floor.

"It's one thing to stuff a rabbit," Lucia cried. "But a cat! That's barbaric!"

"Look at his toes!" Otto said. "On his right front. He's got"—he squinted to see if he was correct—"yes, he's got eight of them!"

"He can't have," Max said. "The most they can have is seven."

"Look!" Otto said, tapping on the window.

At that moment two things happened. The cat looked up, and a voice from within the store called out, "Have you brought me a body? If not, go away!"

The children stared at one another in silence, eyes wide. In a moment they heard a scuffling from within, then the *thunk* of something hitting the floor.

"I think we should leave," Max whispered.

"Nonsense," Lucia said, her voice full of excitement. "He asked about a body. Here's murder at least!"

"He's a taxidermist. He meant an animal's body, I'm sure," Max said.

There was the sharp snap of a lock being turned, and the door was yanked open by a great boulder of a man holding a knife with a long leather strap on the bottom. The front of his body was covered with a slick black apron, and his hair, which was a strawberry blond color, was tied back in a tight braid that reached his shoulder blades. He had a powerful nose and a chin that looked like it could hammer a nail into concrete. If he were wearing an iron helmet, Lucia mused, he would look just like a Viking.

"Well, what do you want?" He swung his knife by its leather strap and tucked it in his back pocket, which thrilled Lucia, since it made him look more like a Viking than ever. Otto and Max, however, had stepped back a pace when he swung the knife.

"My brother was just admiring your cat," Lucia said, nodding toward Otto.

"My cat?" he said, perplexed.

"The one in the window," Lucia said.

The man looked. "Oh, him." His expression softened a little, which only meant that he looked slightly less likely to smash someone on the head with a crowbar. "You in the market for a cat, mate?" he asked Otto.

Otto blinked and looked away.

"Doesn't he talk?" the man asked Lucia.

"No," Lucia said.

"Good. I reckon most people have nothing to say and keep on saying it."

"He was admiring his toes, really," Lucia said.

"Yeah? Well, he ought to!" the man nodded. "He's got twenty-five of them."

"Twenty-one," Max corrected.

The man cocked his massive head to one side and surveyed Max contemptuously. "What are you, an accountant?"

"Eight on the right front, five on the left, and four each on the back. That's twenty-one," Max said.

"Yeah? And what about the fifth leg?" the man said.

The Hardscrabbles eyed the man with disappointment. They never enjoyed it when adults playfully lied to them. The adults always think they're being amusing and imaginative, just like children. But kids never lie playfully. They lie as if their lives depended on it.

"Thank you, good night," Lucia said, and they began to turn away.

"Hang on," the man said, and he ducked back into the store. They watched as he reached into the window and roughly scooped up the cat, who responded to the treatment with a yowl of reproach. The man reappeared at the door and held the cat out, one thick butcher hand cupping the cat's armpits.

"What do you call this then?" He flicked two fingers at a strange appendage hanging off of the cat's left hind leg. The children stepped in closer for a better look. Indeed, it did appear to be the bottom portion of a cat's leg, claws and all. A price tag had been ignominiously attached to the thing by a string, with twenty pounds scrawled on it.

Lucia snorted, her nostrils flaring out especially wide. "It's a trick," she said. "You've attached it."

"Damn you for saying so!!" he cried (in your head, those words sounded very fierce, didn't they? On account of the double exclamation points and the "damn." But really, he said them with less anger than you just imagined).

"Actually, Lucia, it's real," Max said, his fingers examining the cat's appendage.

"Of course it's real! Why wouldn't it be?" the man said.

"The wild boar's tusks aren't," Lucia said.

Here, the man (his name is Saint George, so let's just call him that. I don't want to keep saying "the man" when I know he will be in this book for a while). Here, Saint George realized he was dealing with some shrewd children. He didn't bother denying the wild boar's tusks. Instead, he pointed up at the sign in front of the store.

"It says taxidermy and curiosities, doesn't it?" he said. "Well, that's one of the curiosities. This here cat with five legs is another." He turned his attention to Otto who was staring at the cat's fifth leg with particular interest.

"A connoisseur of the curious, are you?" Saint George nodded approvingly. "Tell you what. Ten pounds and she's yours. I'll even throw in the collar."

"We've got dozens of cats at home," Max said very sensibly.

"But they don't have five legs," Otto said dreamily.

"I said no," Max stated firmly, just as though he were the boss of Otto.

This annoyed Lucia, who was the actual boss of Otto, so she said to Saint George, "Five pounds, we don't care about the collar. Plus you tell us how to get to Haddie Piggit's house."

"Haddie Piggit? What do you want with her?" Saint George said. There was something about the way he said "Haddie Piggit" that interested Lucia. There was a hint of nervousness. What sort of old lady could make a Viking nervous? Lucia wondered.

"We've come to visit her," Max said to Saint George, and to Lucia he said, "Five pounds? We're not wasting what little money we have on a cat."

"You've come to visit and she hasn't told you where she lives?" Saint George said.

"It's a surprise visit," Max said truthfully.

"Do you know her well?" Lucia said.

"No," Saint George said. "She hasn't lived here very long. Came in my shop to ask for some marshmallow rubbish. To spread on bread. Fluffie-something. Said she thought it might count as a curiosity, since no one in this bloody country seems to eat it." Saint George shook his head for a moment, a half smirk on his face. Then his face grew severe again. "You sure she'll want to see you lot?"

"Of course she will," Max said. "She's our great-aunt."

"Really?" He looked at them with confusion. Then he shrugged his enormous shoulders. "All right, if you say so. Let's see the seven pounds—"

"Five," Lucia corrected.

"Seven, and I'll haul you over to her place myself."

"Deal," Lucia said.

Otto dug the notes out of his wallet and handed them to Saint George. Saint George put the notes in his apron pocket, then handed the cat over to Otto.

"Wait here," he ordered them.

The cat adjusted himself in Otto's arms, settling in as though he were curling into a favorite spot on the sofa. His fifth leg draped over the crook of Otto's arm in such a limp, trusting way that Otto made a humming sound, not unlike the satisfied purr of a mother cat.

They waited and waited for Saint George to reappear. While they waited, they listened to the sound of bugs plinking against the streetlight. Then they shared a stick of Such Fun Peppermint gum that Max found in the back pocket of his jeans. Then they spit the gum out because a stick of gum split three ways is worse than no gum at all. They waited and waited, until it became clear that they had been tricked in some way. Saint George must have had a good laugh at their expense and gone to bed. They were just beginning to feel awkward and stupid, which made them cross their arms over their chests, when they heard a *tip-top-tip-top* coupled with a fearsome metallic rattle. They kept very still, listening, and wondering that the entire town hadn't jumped out of their beds and into the street to see what was happening. In a minute, two small, stout white ponies appeared on the side street, pulling a peculiar long rectangular carriage. The carriage was so low to the ground that it almost looked like an elaborate play carriage. It had long panes of glass on either side, on which was painted, in gold letters, SAINT GEORGE'S TAXIDERMY & CURIOSITIES, along with an address and phone number, and below that the words GET STUFFED!

Perched on the driver's box seat and holding the reins was Saint George himself. He halted the ponies with a flick of his wrist and ordered the Hardscrabbles to "Pile in the back and be quick." So the children opened a small door in the back of the carriage and scrambled in. There were no seats in the little carriage. They had to sit on the floor, their backs against the long glass panes. They had barely settled in when the carriage lurched forward and the ponies set off at a frantic trot. They passed through the streets, clattering and tip-topping, and in a few minutes they had left the town entirely and were once again on a country road. The moon had slid out from beneath the clouds, casting gloomy shadows across the fields.

"Strange that there are no seats in this old thing, don't you think?" Lucia said.

"It's not meant for people to sit in," Max said. "It's meant for people to lie down in."

"Nonsense," Lucia said.

"*You're* nonsense," Max said.

"That's a stupid thing to say! Sometimes you act like such an infant." She snorted and things might have gotten ugly but Otto's hands were moving, so Lucia and Max stopped arguing to see what he was saying.

"Who would want to *lie down* in a carriage?" Otto asked.

"Yes, that's what I'd like to know," Lucia said, looking back at Max.

"A dead person would," Max said.

There was a long pause during which Lucia and Otto took in this information. They gazed around at the low-ceilinged carriage and at the heavy black drapes on the two side windowpanes. Max waited.

"It's a funeral carriage?" Lucia said.

"Obviously," Max said, which was obnoxious and he knew it.

You would think that since Lucia loved adventures and Otto loved curiosities, riding in a funeral carriage would have made them ecstatic. But actually it made them very squeamish. To make matters worse, the carriage suddenly picked up speed and they were all violently jostled in a very humiliating way.

"Don't you think it's cruel to make those little ponies pull us along?" Otto said, staring out the front window, past Saint George's back and at the trotting ponies.

"Not as cruel as killing one and stuffing it to make it look like a miniature zebra," Max said, watching the ponies thoughtfully.

"No! He wouldn't have!" Lucia cried. But even as she said it, she realized that it might be true. The ponies did look exactly like that zebra, only without the stripes. And stripes could always be painted on.

"Do you think he planned on killing the cat as well?" Otto asked, holding him a little tighter in his arms.

"I guess a stuffed curiosity is no different from a live one," Max said. "And you wouldn't have to feed it or change the litter."

"That's fiendish!" Lucia cried.

The carriage ride now took on a whole different aspect for the Hardscrabbles. Each one considered how idiotic they had been in accepting a ride from a stranger, especially a stranger who didn't even bother to hide the fact that he was a nasty brute. He had even come to the door with a knife in his hand, hadn't he? What on earth had they been thinking!?

It was Lucia, though, who had suggested they stay and talk to him. And it was Lucia who had agreed to let him take them to their great-aunt Haddie. All three Hardscrabbles remembered this at the same time. Max and Otto turned to glare at their sister, while Lucia flared her nostrils very extravagantly to show that she would not accept the blame for this catastrophe. But secretly she felt awful and her mind was full of grisly visions of three hastily dug graves.

The moon slipped back behind the clouds and the trees on the edge of the road grew taller and pressed together more closely, blotting out the view on either side. Up ahead, the frantic hoofbeats of the white ponies seemed to be rushing the Hardscrabbles to their doom.

Adventures work in peculiar ways, Lucia now thought. You wished and wished for one, then suddenly, without even knowing how, you were in one. It was just as exhilarating as you imagined it would be from the novels. Until something happened, like a nighttime ride in a funeral carriage and the murder of a little white pony. Then you forgot all about the novels, and instead remembered the news stories about unfortunate kids who ended up decapitated in the woods.

"Do you think we could jump?" Lucia asked Max.

He shook his head decisively, as though he'd already considered it. "Too dangerous."

So they once again felt stupid, as well as in terrible danger.

Suddenly, the road dipped down sharply and they slid forward along the black varnished floor. The ponies picked up their pace, and the Hardscrabbles braced their trainers against the floor to keep themselves steady. Even the cat, which had been sleeping soundly through much of the ride, raised its head from the crook of Otto's arm and gazed out at the black blur of trees on either side. It seemed like a ride the cat had been accustomed to taking, or else he had seen such strange, wild things while in the company of Saint George that nothing surprised him anymore. He sneezed, flicked his tail, and then tucked his head back into Otto's arm.

After a while the road levelled out. The air seeping through the vent at the front of the carriage smelled slightly different. More complicated, like a cool brew of soil and sky and dusky faraway places. The trees thinned out and now they could see a formidable dark shape in the distance. It was too lumpy and large to be a house, yet it wasn't a hill either.

"What do you think it is?" Lucia asked.

"It looks like something that's gone all wrong," Otto said.

Lucia knew exactly what he meant. It had bumps in the wrong places and tilted in odd ways. If it was a house, Lucia thought, it must have been built by a madman.

With a twitch of the reins, Saint George drove the ponies into a sharp left turn and the carriage wheels were now crunching across a rough gravel road. The road wound its way between the trees and in a few minutes it became clear that they were headed directly for the large lumpish thing. At that moment, Lucia did a most uncharacteristic thing. She reached out her arms on either side and wrapped them protectively around the shoulders of her brothers.

Chapter 7

In which the Hardscrabbles discover
a Tyrolean traverse, meet Great-aunt Haddie,
and get spat upon

Even the ponies seemed to want to avoid the huge struc-
ture. As the carriage approached it, the ponies suddenly
swerved off the gravel path and onto a broad meadow, but
Saint George set them straight with a sharp yank on their
reins. Lucia supposed that was a lucky thing too, since the
meadow ended abruptly at what she could only imagine
was a deep cliff. Far below and off in the distance, she
could make out the indolent waves of the sea, churning up
that strange odor she'd detected earlier. Close to, the odor
was sharper and she couldn't decide if it was a good smell
or a foul one, sort of like the smell in a barn.

The shifty moon emerged from under clouds again,
casting a dirty yellow light on the landscape. The large
lumpish thing could now be seen for what it was: a castle
of some sort, though it was nothing like the castles you see

in book illustrations or in the movies. Yes, it had all the parts of a castle, like towers and turrets and a curtain wall that surrounded it, but they were sloppily formed and slapped together. It seemed incredible that such a thing could even stand on its own, but there it was. Even more incredibly, someone was living in it. Lights could be seen in some of the pinchy-narrow windows, mostly on the upper floors.

It was Max who suddenly crawled over to the back of the carriage and swung open the door.

"What are you doing?" Lucia called to him, but he ignored her. Crouching at the edge of the open door, he reached up and grabbed the railing along the roof of the carriage. Then he pulled himself up and stood on the back step so that he was riding outside.

"Excuse me," Max called out to Saint George, "but do you *really* know where Haddie Piggit lives?"

"You're looking at it," Saint George called back without turning his head.

"There?" Max exclaimed. "No, no, I don't think so. Look, why not leave us off right here and we'll find her ourselves."

"Yes! Leave us off!" Lucia screamed. She had scooched up to the back and poked her head out.

"Go back inside before you get tossed on your loaf," Saint George yelled. He then yanked the reins, making the ponies turn to the right so suddenly that Max would have been tossed on his loaf if Lucia hadn't grabbed his legs just in time. She hauled him back inside, leaving the back door open and flapping wildly. They were approaching the front of the castle now. Across the castle moat, they could see the great misshapen lumps of stone. They looked damp, as though they were in a cold sweat. A light from one of the tower rooms flicked off, and there was the distinct sound of a wail, short and high-pitched. Then silence, except for the slap of waves against the cliff and the snorting of the ponies, and finally the thud of the carriage's back door as it slammed shut once again.

"I wish we were back in Little Tunks," Otto said.

In certain novels with eerie castles, they might have suddenly been whisked back to Little Tunks at that very moment, and found themselves snug in their own beds. In fact, at Otto's words, Lucia closed her eyes tightly and on opening them again half-expected to see the face of the Sultan of Juwi staring back at her from his place on her bedroom wall.

Instead, when she opened her eyes, she saw something quite remarkable. In fact, she thought she *was* seeing magic. The huge, lumpy castle had quite suddenly shrunk. It was all there—the towers, the turrets, the curtain wall. Except that it was now the size of one of those fake castles that you find in theme parks.

This book is not about magic, however. When Lucia got her bearings she saw that the real castle was behind them and they were facing a replica, almost like the original castle had given birth to a baby version of itself.

"It's a castle folly," cried Max.

"No, it's not," Lucia said, because she counted herself

the authority on castles, since she read about them so often, and she'd never heard of a castle folly.

The reins were pulled taut and the ponies slowed to a stop.

"Right, out you go!" Saint George called back to them. Out they went.

For a moment, all they felt was relief at not being murdered.

"Mind the moat," was all Saint George said before he flicked the reins against the ponies' backs and drove off.

They stood there for a moment, looking baffled.

"Well, this was a brilliant idea," Lucia said to Max.

"Would you rather be at home with Mrs. Carnival's cyst?" Max replied.

"It doesn't bother *me*," Lucia said.

"Good. Then next time I'll tell her that you want to be the one who drains it."

They argued like this for some time, since it was preferable to actually knocking on the little castle's door and waking up an old lady who might not be happy to see them. And who might have gruesome breath, like old Mr. Abernathy, who stocked the shelves at the supermarket back in Little Tunks.

"What if she won't let Chester in?" Otto said.

"Who's Chester?" Lucia asked.

"The cat. I've named him Chester. What if she won't let him in?"

Chester the cat had been circling Otto's ankles, and now he stopped and looked at the little castle speculatively.

"Then she's a nasty old cow," Lucia declared. She needed a dose of righteous anger to make her braver. So she was the first to march up to the edge of the moat, looking for a way across it.

There wasn't one.

Although this castle was not as big as the first one, the moat was just as wide as the first moat. They did spot a drawbridge, but it was clapped up against the side of the castle.

"We could swim it," Lucia suggested.

"We could, but there's nothing to take hold of once you're across," Max said.

It was true. There was nothing to grip on to by the castle. And though you could jump off the bank into the water, it would be very difficult to climb back up since the bank had such a long, deep drop.

"We could yell for her to let down the drawbridge," Lucia suggested.

So they did. They sounded like a right pack of idiots too. Still, the drawbridge remained up and not a single light came on in the castle.

"Maybe she can't hear very well," Max said.

"Or maybe she's ignoring us," said Lucia, "hoping we'll just go away." She narrowed her eyes at the castle. She felt as though she were being dared. "Wait here," she commanded.

Slowly, she walked the perimeter, examining the steepness of the bank, the sides of the curtain wall, the trees that flanked the moat. There was a very tall wooden tower as well, so tall that it loomed over several of the trees. It was made of crisscrossed timbers, set on wheels. A narrow, rickety-looking ladder was bound to the timbers, leading up to a roofed platform. It was while Lucia was looking up at the platform that she saw something unusual. Dangling high above her head was a bicycle, floating in the night sky, waiting for someone to hop on.

"Bloody hell," she whispered. But as I said before, this is not a book about magic—not the kind you're thinking of anyway—so Lucia came to her senses and asked herself, "How is it that a bicycle *appears* to be floating in the night sky?"

After a careful investigation into the matter, she discovered that the bicycle was attached by hooks to one of two slender cables that ran from the wooden tower all the way across the moat and to the upper part of the castle.

"I've found it!" she called out to her brothers. "I've found a way in!"

They hurried over, Chester jogging alongside, and she pointed up to the bicycle. She didn't explain to them about the cable right away. She wanted them to think it was magic at first, like she had. She understood that even when you don't strictly believe in magic, it's always nice to think it's possible, just for a second.

"It looks exactly like it's enchanted," Otto said, staring up at the bicycle.

"It looks exactly like a Tyrolean traverse," Max said flatly. "In fact, it is one."

"Nonsense," Lucia sniped. "Look, it's attached to a cable. You can ride it straight over the moat."

"Like a Tyrolean traverse," Max muttered.

"In any case"—she lowered her eyelids to half-mast and flared her nostrils at him—"it will get us in the castle. It's attached to the top of that left-hand tower. One of us can slip in the house through the roof and let down the drawbridge for the others."

"Someone's watching us," Otto said suddenly.

"Great-aunt Haddie, do you think?" Max asked.

"No. Someone else." Otto wasn't looking at the little castle, but at the large castle that loomed behind them in the blackness. His eyes were wide with alarm. It made them all feel squirrelly—even Chester stood very still, his tail curled like a question mark—so they told Otto to cut it out.

"I don't know," Max said, staring back up at the bicycle doubtfully, his spidery arms crossed against his chest. "It seems a sneaky way to get into the house."

"You were going to sneak into Angela's house," Lucia pointed out.

"Yes, but she wasn't home at the time," Max said.

"Well, if Great-aunt Haddie didn't want people to use the bicycle, why would she leave it up there in the first place?" Lucia said.

"Maybe she didn't think anyone would be brave enough to try," Max said.

(I'm going to interrupt here to let you know that Lucia was not really fooled by this ploy. She knew that it was Max's way of getting her to be the one to ride the bike over the moat. She knew it subconsciously, so even though it *appeared* that she was tricked, deep down she knew exactly what he was up to.)

"Well, Great-aunt Haddie hasn't met someone like me, has she?" Lucia declared. Then she began to climb the ladder. It was a very rickety ladder. It was a very tall tower. Midway Lucia had to stop climbing for a minute to compose herself and steady her racing heart. It was then that she remembered what Otto had said about someone watching them. She felt it too. Or maybe she just imagined it. Often Otto felt things while she just imagined she felt them.

"All right?" Max called up.

"Of course!" Lucia called back and resumed her climb.

Rung by rung, she made her way to the top of the tower until she was able to step onto the platform. The bicycle was right in front of her now, its back wheel touching the platform's railing. The bike was old and crusted with rust. The tires looked a bit soggy too, though that didn't matter really since she'd be riding on a cable, not on wheels. Lucia looked down at the moat far, far below. It was a nasty drop. If the cable didn't hold, or she lost her balance, the fall would mean several broken bones. If she was lucky.

Courage, Lucia, she told herself. Think of the Sultan of Juwi. Think of how he refused to hide from Dr. Azziz. How he sat on that fountain every day. Now *that* was courage! Surely she could find the courage to cross a silly moat.

Leaning over the railing, she gave the bicycle a downward tug. It seemed secure enough. Carefully, she eased herself over the railing and with one swift movement she lunged forward, catching hold of the handlebars and lowering herself onto the bicycle seat. The bicycle bounced a bit and the cable dipped under her weight.

"Steady on, Lucia!" Max called up. She nodded but didn't look down at him.

Nothing happened for a second. She wondered with some relief if the thing was busted. But then she started to move. It went slowly at first. Above her head she heard the tentative *shiiish*ing sound of the hook rubbing against the cable. But then it picked up speed. A lot of speed. In the space of a few seconds, the bicycle was shooting down the cable alarmingly fast. Lucia held her breath. Her fingers squeezed the handlebars so hard that her knuckles ached, and the wind blew her dark hair into her eyes. It was right about then that she realized her mistake. She had assumed that it would be a fairly tame ride over the moat and the curtain wall; that when the bicycle reached the castle tower, it would be a simple matter of climbing onto the roof. But now she saw that she was going far too fast for a gentle landing. At this rate of speed the front tire of the bicycle would hit the castle wall with such force that she would certainly bounce back violently and be pitched into the moat. Her brain scrambled for solutions, but she could only think of two and neither one was very happy. "Jump now or crash in the wall, jump or crash, jump or crash—"

"Stay put!" a voice called out. It wasn't a voice in her head. It wasn't the voice of either of her brothers. It was a strange voice that seemed to waft by her on a breeze, from a distance off.

So she stayed put, held her breath, and watched as the

stone wall came closer and closer at terrifying speed. A second before the bicycle slammed into the castle wall, Lucia squeezed her eyes shut and screamed (you would have done the same, you know you would!).

Suddenly everything stopped. Even with her eyes closed Lucia was pretty sure she was still on the bicycle and that she was all in one piece, although she had heard about people who had fingers cut off in factory accidents and didn't feel a thing until they saw the blood.

"You might have just knocked on the front door, you know," a voice said from somewhere below her.

Lucia opened her eyes. She was *inside* the castle folly, still sitting on the bicycle but dangling high off the ground. The cable ended in the middle of a round ceiling, right beside a chandelier that was not very clean. Directly below her was a bed. And lying on that bed, gazing up at her, was a young woman. She was dressed in a white T-shirt and black sweatpants, and she held a paperback book in her hands while a package of chocolate biscuits lay in her lap. Her hair was blond and cut very short, like a boy's, and she was slim and slight and narrow-hipped. In fact, if you were nearsighted, you could easily have mistaken her for a self-possessed fourteen-year-old boy.

"How did I get inside?" Lucia asked, looking around dazedly.

"Through the window, of course." The young woman nodded her small round chin toward a pair of curtains across from the bed. They were made of a heavy grey fabric. The sort of fabric that, on dark murky nights, probably looked an awful lot like a solid block of stone wall. "Good thing it was open."

It was at this point that Lucia began to feel awkward. It's one thing to ride a bike through someone's window and helplessly dangle from their ceiling. But it's quite another thing to have that somebody stare up at you nonchalantly, while eating chocolate biscuits in their bed, as though you were a funny circus act. In fact, the woman appeared to be waiting for Lucia's next trick.

"You might help me to get down," Lucia said with annoyance.

"You don't need any help. Just jump," the woman said. "You'll land on the bed, unless you're a total klutz."

Now Lucia began to suspect three things: one, that the woman was not British. She had a funny, nasally way of talking, which Lucia guessed was an American accent; two, that the woman probably had ridden on the bike herself more than once; and three, that Lucia had better jump onto the bed immediately or she would look like a yellow-bellied coward.

So she jumped and landed pretty squarely in the center of the bed. The woman must have known that's where she'd land, because she'd already bent her knees and pulled her legs back while protectively holding the package of biscuits up in one hand.

"Well done," the woman said. "Have an Oreo," and she offered Lucia a chocolate biscuit. That seemed too much like a treat offered to a circus monkey, so Lucia declined, nostrils flared, then scooted off the bed.

"You're very uppity for someone who just broke into my home," the woman said, taking a bite out of the Oreo that Lucia had refused.

"I didn't break in. We tried to get in the normal way but your bridge was up and we yelled and yelled—"

"Oh, are there more of you?" The woman sat up a little straighter in bed as though the situation was getting more interesting by the minute. The fact that she was so unruffled by all this ruffled Lucia even more and she forgot to ask the most obvious question, which you are probably already asking in your own head.

"There are three of us. Otto and Max are standing on the other side of the moat, waiting for me to let them in—"

"Is that how you operate? One breaks in and then lets in the others? Clever. I'm guessing that one of your brothers is a big ugly bruiser who will smash me on the head with a shovel, while the other one, the rat-faced one with waxy ears, will rifle through all my stuff, looking for the valuables."

Lucia could only stare at this odd woman in confusion until she finally gathered up her wits to object: "They don't have waxy ears or shovels or anything like that. They're nice looking, for your information."

"Well, they would be. Your dad was good looking, as I remember. And your mom was always—" The woman stopped here. Suddenly, she looked a little uncomfortable. "Your mom was a peach."

Now Lucia thought of the question that she should have asked a few minutes ago, and the one that you have already asked in your head: "You aren't Great-aunt Haddie, are you?"

"I am," the woman replied.

"But you're too young," Lucia said.

"How good are you at math?"

"Pretty good," Lucia said. In fact she was appallingly bad at math.

"Your great-grandmother had me when she was fifty-two. My oldest sister was thirty-one years older than me. By the time I was born, my sister had a three-year-old daughter. That was your mother. I was her aunt, even though I was a baby. That makes me your great-aunt. Got it?"

Lucia nodded yes, even though she didn't. There was a silence during which Lucia was trying to do the math.

"Don't you think you should let your brothers in?" Haddie asked.

Lucia nodded again, but still sat there, frowning and thinking.

Haddie leapt out of bed. "Lucia, isn't it?" She even pronounced it right.

"Yes."

Haddie pulled on a dressing gown that was flung across an oval standing mirror. "Come on. I'll show you how to lower the drawbridge."

She led Lucia through a narrow stone hallway, lit by wall sconces, and down several twisting staircases. Everything was much smaller than it should have been. Even the ceilings were so low that a tallish adult would have had to duck while walking through the halls. Luckily, Haddie was hardly taller than Otto, so they navigated fairly comfortably. Haddie led Lucia through an impressive-looking oak door banded and studded with iron, though not nearly as tall as a normal door, and outside into a courtyard. Straight ahead was a gatehouse, the opening of which was barred by a portcullis. Though Lucia had never seen an actual portcullis, she suspected that this one was on the puny side. In her books, it often took several large, grunting men to raise the portcullis and let down the drawbridge but Haddie managed it all very easily without any grunting at all. The drawbridge creaked down on its pulleys and landed with a solid thump.

"Be you friends or foes!?" Haddie called out to the two nervous-looking shadows on the far side of the moat.

Lucia thought that was a nice touch.

"Friends!" Max called back.

"Excellent! Proceed! And watch out for the crocodile in the moat!" Haddie called back.

"Is there really?" Lucia asked her.

"No. But I'm considering getting one. Do you think it could survive in an English moat?"

"I think they're rather tropical animals."

"Ooo, *rather*!" Haddie replied, and Lucia had the uncomfortable feeling that Haddie was making fun of her.

"Hello!" Haddie stepped forward as the boys came across to the other side. "You're Otto, and you must be Max."

Otto and Max shot a questioning glance at Lucia.

"She's Great-aunt Haddie," Lucia said, happy to have the correct information before Max did. "It makes sense if you do the math," she assured them, even though she still didn't understand it.

"Do you know that your shirt is squirming?" Haddie asked Otto.

Otto nodded sheepishly.

"You should let it out, don't you think?" Haddie said.

So Otto pulled Chester out from under his shirt.

"Now let's get down to business." Haddie looked at them all with her hands planted on her boy hips, her brows pinched into a serious frown. But it wasn't like most adults' serious frowns. It was like she was imitating a serious frown. "Does your father know you're here?"

They considered lying to her, because they all, quite suddenly, wanted very badly to stay. But before they did, Haddie answered for them.

"No, of course he doesn't know," she said. "He'd have never let you come here in the first place."

"Really? Why not?" Max asked.

"Because . . ." Haddie squinted at them, then shifted her legs uneasily. She sucked air into her mouth, and worked her jaw around in a peculiar way, as though she were considering how to answer. Then she blew a spitball right into Max's eye.

"Hey!" Max clapped his hand to his eye.

"Oh, sorry about that," Haddie said blandly. She pivoted on her bare feet and said, "Onward and inward," then headed back through the courtyard toward the house.

The Hardscrabbles looked at one another for a moment. It was possible that the spitball was an accident.

That she just meant to blow off an expressive *phew* and the spit simply rode on an innocent air stream directly into Max's eye. But they all suspected that it was deliberate and still do, especially now that they know *why* their father didn't want them to come visit her.

They followed her anyway. You would have too.

Chapter 8

In which the Hardscrabbles gag on
peanut butter and jelly and then are locked in the dungeon,
where Max begins to think deeply and importantly

In the main entranceway, the Hardscrabbles gawked at a child-size suit of armor before Haddie led them down a corridor with heavy timber beams running across the ceiling and narrow arched windows set deep into the lumpy stone wall. The Hardscrabbles' collective trainers made an awful squeaky sound against the floor as they passed several small alcoves that half hid spiralling staircases.

"Here we are," Haddie said, and led them into a small round room that was a kitchen of some sort. It had a little pink play oven that reached no higher than Lucia's hip, as well as a tiny pink play refrigerator. There was a real sink, though much squatter than a normal one. In the middle of the room was a small pink plastic table with four tiny pink chairs, the backs of which were shaped like hearts. Haddie nodded toward it.

"Sit. Hungry?"

They were. Haddie opened the tiny play refrigerator and looked inside. There couldn't have been much in there, but still she stared inside thoughtfully for quite a while. Finally, she pulled out two jars of something or other and a loaf of bread. Using a pink plastic knife, Haddie slathered the bread with the contents of the jars, then handed each of the children a sandwich on pink plastic tea saucers.

The last time they had eaten had been at the Indian restaurant, so they all bit into the sandwiches eagerly. After a few chews, however, they all pulled faces of disgust and swallowed with difficulty. Haddie was watching them, fascinated.

"Don't like it, do you?" she asked happily.

"What is it?" Max asked.

"Peanut butter and jelly."

"Jelly?" Lucia wrinkled her nose. "You mean that wiggly stuff?"

"She means jam," Max said; then explaining to Haddie, "Our jelly is Jell-O." He opened up the sandwich now and studiously examined the gloppy mess inside. "Americans love this stuff, don't they?"

"And British people don't, huh?" Haddie raised one eyebrow and nodded significantly. "Makes you think, doesn't it?"

"It does," Max agreed. He loved to think. In fact, he went so far as to take another bite of the repulsive sandwich so as to think more about it.

"Do you have anything else to eat?" Lucia asked, looking around the kitchen doubtfully.

"I've got canned soup. Loads of canned soup. In case there's a siege. Do British people like soup?" Haddie said.

They told her that they did. She opened the oven door and pulled out two cans of soup and a can opener. Then she opened a box that was sitting on top of the little refrigerator. The top of the box said Young Mad Scientist and had a picture of a boy with dishevelled hair wearing a lab coat and holding a test tube. From inside the box, Haddie pulled out a Bunsen burner, two test tubes, and a box of matches. After flipping a lever on the bottom of the Bunsen burner, she struck a match. The burner began to hiss and when Haddie touched the match to the air above the barrel, a blue flame shot out. She opened up the can of soup and carefully poured it into the test tube. Then, with a pair of tongs clamped around the tube, she held it over the flame and the soup began to cook.

"This is a castle folly, isn't it?" Max said.

"That's what they told me when I rented it," Haddie said.

"Oh, for goodness' sakes, what on earth is a castle folly?" Lucia asked in a very irritated tone.

"It's a sort of play castle," Max answered.

"It's exactly a play castle," Haddie said.

The Bunsen burner cooked the soup rather rapidly, which was a good thing considering that Haddie had to cook six test tubes full of soup in order to feed them all. As she did, she told them about the castle folly.

"The castle across the way, Kneebone Castle, is very, very old, built in the 1300s for Lord and Lady Kneebone. Apparently the Kneebones liked to have loads of kids but didn't enjoy being around them. They built this folly for the kids to live in, with their own servants and tutors and enough to do so that they wouldn't bug their parents. Nice, huh? Anyway, generations of Kneebone kids have grown up here. The last bunch were real pigs. I spent the first few days here digging filthy socks out of the garden hose and scraping gum off the floor. But it's a castle, hey? I always wanted to live in a castle, ever since I was a kid. I can't afford a real one, but I could afford to rent a fake one for the summer. And I was told that there are hidden tunnels and a secret passageway."

"So this place doesn't have any history, then?" Lucia asked. "No bloody battles or poisoned goblets or anything?"

"Nah. Not here in the folly," Haddie said as she tipped a test tube of soup into Otto's pink plastic bowl. "Now if it's tales of blood and gore that you're after, the Kneebone Castle across the way is—" She stopped as though she remembered something.

"What?" Lucia asked eagerly.

"What?" Haddie responded blankly.

"You were going to say something."

"No, I wasn't." She stared back at Lucia challengingly. "But *you* were just about to tell me why, at half-past midnight, you've all suddenly arrived at my home."

"No, I wasn't," Lucia said.

"Well, don't you think it's time you did?" Haddie said.

So they told her the whole story, and she listened beautifully. While she listened, she pulled her feet up on her chair and picked at a scab on her ankle. She picked at it until it bled, but she was so interested in the story she didn't even notice. She looked admiringly at the Hardscrabbles during the parts about Frog Nose and taking the ride from Saint George, though Lucia may have exaggerated the element of danger just a bit.

When Lucia was finished, Haddie sat in silence for a moment. They thought she was most probably contemplating their bravery and quick-thinking. Finally she said, "I have one question."

Lucia nodded eagerly. She loved talking about the day, because all in all it sounded like a tremendous adventure.

But Haddie's gaze slid over to Otto. "What I want to know is why you don't remove your scarf?"

The question took them all by surprise. It had been many years since someone had asked Otto that question.

"He won't answer you. He doesn't talk," Lucia said.

Haddie ignored her and kept looking straight at Otto. "Come on," she said to him. "What's up with the scarf thing, Slick?"

There was a long silence while Haddie waited for Otto to answer. He looked away, stroked the cat in his lap, fiddled with his scarf, then went back to eating his soup. But beneath his overgrown hair, his eyes were scooting around nervously. Still, Haddie waited. It was unbearable for Lucia, who was used to answering for Otto promptly.

"He just really likes his scarf, that's all," Lucia said finally.

Haddie leaned across the table so that her face was inches from Otto. In a quiet voice she said, "We know better, don't we, pal?"

Otto looked up from his soup, startled. He opened his mouth as though he were about to say something. Lucia's and Max's eyes grew wide. Then he shut his mouth again.

"It's late," Haddie announced. "Finish up the soup, then time for bed. And seeing as you are invaders in my castle, I think I'll put you in the dungeon. You don't mind dungeons, do you?"

It was hard to say since they'd never been in one. But Lucia, at least, thought it sounded gruesome, so she said, "Not at all. We like them actually."

Haddie gave them T-shirts and shorts to wear for pyjamas and a tube of toothpaste, but they had to use their fingers for that since their toothbrushes were back at the willow tree. In a real castle the restroom was just a hole in the floor, called a garderobe, and all the nasty stuff fell through a hole and out onto the ground or in the moat. Thankfully, this castle had a real restroom, though it was so tiny you had to keep your arms close to your side or you'd hit the walls.

Afterwards, Haddie led them back out through the hallway, down one of the dark, winding stairwells, and into a room with bare stone walls and one slitty little window high up the wall with a iron grill over it. Hanging from the ceiling by chains were three pallets with thin mattresses on them. While the Hardscrabbles had been changing and brushing their teeth, Haddie had put out some blankets and pillows on the beds.

"Try to keep still-ish during the night," Haddie said.

"Why?" Max asked.

"Because if you keep still, *they* will too." Haddie walked to the door and then turned back. "You'll stay for a while, won't you? You won't skedaddle back home tomorrow?"

"Our dad won't be back for several days," Max said. "We have nowhere else to go." (Not quite true.)

"Excellent," Haddie said.

Then she shut the dungeon door. And bolted it. The Hardscrabbles weren't too happy about that part. Still, as Lucia said, what was the point of sleeping in a dungeon if the door was left unlocked?

"What do you think *they* are? The things that will keep still if we do?" Max asked.

"You're scared, aren't you?" Lucia asked. She didn't ask this in a taunting way. She asked this in a hopeful way, because it's always more satisfying to be brave when someone else is afraid. Especially if it's someone who is occasionally braver than you are.

"Not exactly. I'm just slightly . . . restive," Max said.

"That's crap. You're as nervous as a pigeon," Lucia said.

"That's what I said," said Max.

"No, you didn't. You just said you were tired," Lucia replied.

There was silence in the room. Dungeons are exactly as dark as you think they would be, by the way.

"Restive doesn't mean *tired*," Max said finally. "It means nervous."

It does actually. I looked it up later. However, I wouldn't advise using that word because it will only annoy people, and they will think you are a giant-size prat.

Otto sat down on one of the pallets, making the chain squeal a bit. Right after there was a sound of something skittering across the floor and up the wall. Startled, Lucia and Max leapt up on a pallet too—the same one—and the skittering continued for a few seconds more. Chester was the only one who thought it was a good idea to see what was crawling about. He had bounded off Otto's lap and was running around on the floor, chasing something that they could not see in the blackness. He didn't catch it, because he jumped back in Otto's lap and there was nothing hanging out of his mouth. The fifth leg probably slowed him down.

"I guess that was the *they* she was talking about," Max said when all went quiet again.

"Otto?" Lucia asked. Through the darkness, she could see his scared, pale face staring back at her. "It's okay. It's probably just mice."

"Crawling up the wall?" Max said.

Lucia punched him in the thigh.

"Let's just go to sleep," Lucia said. She jumped off the pallet and climbed into the empty one. Suddenly they heard the skittering again, fast and furious. This time it seemed to come from the opposite side of the room, crawling down the wall and across the floor, then back up the wall. Chester leapt off Otto's lap and chased the thing again, making a flying leap for it as it climbed the wall, then landing on his side with a thump. After that, he stood vigil by the wall, waiting for it to skitter back down again.

"Did you hear what she said about underground tunnels and secret passageways?" Lucia said, for Otto's sake mostly, to keep his mind off the thing in the room. "Tomorrow we should explore."

Otto nodded, but Max only replied, "Hnnn?"

"We should explore, I said," Lucia repeated.

"Right," Max said, but he sounded preoccupied. He was thinking deeply and importantly. Lucia knew from experience not to interrupt him when he was thinking deeply and importantly. If you let him alone, he would eventually tell you something very interesting.

Finally, he said, "I was just thinking about Haddie."

"What about her?" Lucia asked.

"Did you notice something odd about her?" Max said.

"Well, she's awfully young for a great-aunt, but it works out if you do the math," Lucia said (though she still hadn't been able to).

"No, no, not that," Max said.

"She seems lonely," Lucia said. "She really wanted us to stay."

"Maybe," Max said. "But that isn't it."

Max could be infuriatingly slow to come to the point sometimes. Lucia was forced to lean across and smack him on the head with her pillow. "Oh, for goodness' sakes, could you just tell us already?"

"Ow! You didn't need to do that, you know," he said.

The skittering started up again, and this time Lucia saw the thing. Her eyes must have adjusted to the dark. It was a rat. Quite large and running down the wall. A noise came out of her mouth that Max says was a shriek but really it was just a gasp of surprise, with some extra sound to it.

They all sat up in bed then and watched the rat race along the bottom of the floor, with Chester right behind it, then up the wall. It went straight up, like a spider, all the way until it disappeared into the ceiling. Chester sat by the wall and stared up, his tail curled into a question mark.

"Rats can't climb walls," Lucia whispered.

"I know," Max whispered back.

Suddenly he jumped up on his bed noisily and leapt off of it, then rushed to the center of the room. The sound of skittering started up and sure enough, the rat was climbing back down the wall. This time Chester crouched low and pounced just as the rat hit the ground. But the rat flew out from between his claws, apparently unhurt, and shot across the floor again. With a leap, Max threw his whole body down on the creature, much to Lucia's disgust and awe. He stayed on the ground for a few moments, holding the rat beneath him with great difficulty. The creature was crying out with a strange whining sound, until it shot out from beneath him and hurried back across the floor and up the wall.

"I can't believe you did that!" Lucia cried. "Did it bite you?"

"Oh, for heaven's sake, Lucia. Don't you *see*?"

"No."

"This isn't a real castle. Or a real dungeon. Or a real rat. It's a toy. Spring-loaded, I think, and it's triggered by the bed chains' movement. It runs on a little track."

So the Hardscrabbles spent the next twenty minutes jumping on their beds and making the rat run across the floor, behaving exactly the same way that generations of Kneebone children had behaved in the dungeon, until poor Chester looked like he would collapse from heart failure.

Thus, they all forgot about the strange thing that Max had noticed about Haddie. All but Max, of course, who lay awake in bed long after the others had gone to sleep, thinking deeply and importantly.

Chapter 9

In which the Hardscrabbles worry
about the title of this book and other things

The thing that's been bothering me about this book so far is that we all seem very ordinary. A few times I tried to make us sound more dashing and heroic, but one of us (I won't say who, but I bet you know) made me take those parts out because they weren't factual. He said that we started off ordinary and *became* remarkable because of everything that happened, and people need to know the truth.

"The truth is a slippery fish," I replied.

"You don't even know what that means," he said.

"You can bloody well stuff it," I told him.

Things got ugly after that.

The other thing that's been bothering me is that we haven't yet mentioned The Kneebone Boy and he is the title of this book. That seems like a serious flaw. Still, it can't be helped because that's the way things worked out, and anyway he's coming in very soon. We're not overly worried about *you* in particular, because we're guessing that the castle folly and our missing mum is enough to keep you happy for a while. We are slightly worried about Mr. Dupuis, however, who might have some harsh things to say about sloppy plotting.

Chapter 10

In which the Hardscrabbles find out some things about their mother, Max eats a Pixy Stix, and then makes Otto angry

It was hard to tell when it was morning. There was only the sliver of a window with the iron grill over it and it was way high up on the wall. If the day was overcast, as it was that morning, the dungeon was nearly as dark as it was in the middle of the night.

Chester was the first to get up. He stretched out his supple black body, then sat on top of Otto's chest and cleaned himself thoroughly, paying special attention to his fifth leg.

The Hardscrabbles all did essentially the same thing, but it took them a lot longer. They stretched and groaned, their bodies cramped from the thin mattresses. They stared at one another dumbly for a while, silently putting together the events from yesterday.

"We ought to ring Mrs. Carnival," Otto said. "In case

Dad rings her looking for us when he can't get through to Angela."

Max shook his head. "She'll make us go back to Little Tunks."

"We can just tell her that we're all right."

"You *know* she'll ask questions," Max droned.

"If she does, we'll just hang up."

It was the right and responsible thing to do, so they put it off until later.

Max wanted to explore the castle folly, but Lucia was anxious to look at the sea. She had felt the sea tugging at her since they'd first arrived. It gave her a sloshy feeling between her ears.

Much to their surprise, the dungeon door was unlocked. In fact, they discovered that it didn't lock at all, it only made a sound like it was being bolted shut when you closed it. They all used the restroom until they were reasonably clean and since Haddie was nowhere to be found, they decided to go directly to the seaside.

Outside, the air was already warming and all around was the smell of the sea. A rolling carpet of fog concealed everything below their knees, so that often all they could see of Chester was the top of his question-mark tail. A combination of the sea smell and the fog gave Lucia the delicious sense of time collapsing. She imagined that she could hear the cannon fire of great ships of war, the splash of Viking oars, even the slow-motion footsteps of dinosaurs pressing through primordial forests.

Their walk toward the sea took them right past

Kneebone Castle. In the daylight, it was even uglier than it had appeared the night before. Its stones were an oily-looking brown, fat and lumpy and uneven, like enormously thick hamburger patties stacked on top of each other. Only the windows and crenellations were neatly hewn out of the stone. The drawbridge was up and the portcullis was down.

"What an awful-looking place," Lucia said, gazing up at the towers. She was enchanted. "Do you think it's open to the public?"

"I'm sure it's not," Max said.

"How do you know?" Lucia said, winching her brows at him.

"The curtain wall has been patched up recently," Max said. "Look along the top."

Sure enough there was a smooth rim of stone along the top of the wall that did not quite match the hamburger stone. It was paler and the lichen hadn't mottled its surface.

"So?" Lucia said.

"And the crenellations on the castle's towers are all crumbly."

"And I repeat . . . so?"

"That means someone cared more about keeping people out than impressing people who might come in." He paused. Then he added, "It's just a guess, though. I may be completely wrong."

He always said that when he knew he was 100 percent right.

Otto had been staring up at the castle, squinting. As

they walked he kept turning around to see something up in one of the towers.

"What?" Lucia said finally.

Otto stopped walking and took one long look up at the castle. "The tower on the right. Third window from the top."

They looked. They squinted. Then they saw it. There was a figure in one of the windows. It was hard to see the person very clearly at that distance, and the fog that drifted in front of their faces periodically made it even harder, but it appeared that he or she was staring straight back at them.

Max waved. The person did not wave back. They just kept staring.

"What if she's being held prisoner?" Lucia said hopefully.

"Then she probably would have waved back," Max said. "And it might be a he."

"Ha! Not likely," Lucia said. "Didn't you notice them?"

"Them what?" Max asked.

"Her . . . you know. She has breasts, Max! What do you think that is on her chest?"

"I think it's a pair of crossed arms," Max said.

It was. Most probably.

Otto laughed, a little pop of air that sounded like a pickle jar being opened.

So Lucia temporarily lost interest in the person at the tower window and quickened her pace toward the water.

Soon they came to the edge of the cliff, which dropped down at an alarmingly steep angle to a shingle beach far below. The beach was now receiving a fine thrashing from the white-tipped waves, and the whole view—the sky, as slickery as blue rain boots, the rippling water, the milk white triangle of a taut sail on a distant boat—was all too gaspingly perfect. They stared at it for a while (during which Lucia thought up the blue rain boot description) until they became bored. So they looked for a way down.

There wasn't one. The castle was perched on the very edge of a precipice, as castles often are, to keep off the foreign invaders. Installing a set of stairs from the cliff to the beach would naturally be counterproductive. What they did find, or rather what Otto found, was a perilously jagged path that more or less led down to the beach. It required some creative thinking to figure out how they were supposed to get from one ledge to the next when the two might be a good distance apart, but they did it, and suffered only minor abrasions and a tiny amount of blood loss.

Lucia and Max chucked their shoes and socks and chased the waves. Then they let the waves chase them as they ran backwards on the narrow strip of sand. It made them laugh like infants.

Otto, however, sat close to the edge of the cliff face and examined the smooth stones that covered most of the beach. Chester stayed with him, though Lucia could have sworn Chester was watching the waves with the most wistful expression.

"Come on!" Lucia called to Otto. "The water feels gorgeous on your ankles!"

But Otto refused until Lucia finally relented and left Max to chase the waves by himself. She ran over to Otto, still laughing, and collapsed on the ground beside him. She smiled at him but he didn't notice. He was absently examining a white-streaked stone that he held in his palm. He was so solemn. So *sad*. Was he always like that and she had never noticed? It bothered her, especially because she had just felt the wonderful blood rush that comes from being silly and barefoot.

"When I grow up," she said, because it was their special game, and she wanted him to stop looking at the stupid stone, "I'll buy a lighthouse by the sea, for us to live in. At night we'll watch for ships that are about to crash into the cliffs and we'll shine the lights and save them. During the day we can throw things down at people on the beach."

Otto balanced the stone on his knee and said nothing, just stared at it.

"What's wrong with you?" She grabbed the stupid stone out of his hand and threw it as far as she could. Then she felt bad.

Otto stared after the lost stone, then looked at Lucia. There was something he wanted to tell her, something important. She kept very still, her eyes on his eyes, waiting. Then he turned away from her. He picked up another stone, one with black speckles, and began to examine it.

That was when Lucia first began to suspect that Otto was keeping a secret. A big fat one.

They had spent several hours by the water, and had even discovered a cave, in which they looked for evidence of an old pirate hideout but all they found were some empty

Coke cans and a vintage car magazine. By noonish, though, they were getting hungry and headed back to the castle folly. On the way back they looked for the person in the tower at Kneebone Castle but there was no one at the window now. The castle was so still and silent that they stood there for a few minutes, looking up at it.

Have you ever stared at someone while they were sleeping, and then realized that they were not asleep at all but were lying there with their eyes opened in slits, staring right back at you? It gives you a very squirrelly feeling. It was the same thing with Kneebone Castle. The Hardscrabbles suddenly all got the feeling that it was watching them through its arrow slits. Otto was first to start backing away from the place, then Lucia and Max did as well, and they hurried back over the meadow to the castle folly as fast as they could without actually running.

"Ho! Prisoners!" a voice called down from somewhere above them as they approached the folly's moat. They looked along the walkway on top of the curtain wall, but they didn't see a single thing.

The person whistled. It was a very loud and impressive whistle and it directed their attention to a pair of feet in flip-flops resting on the railing of the tall wooden tower that Lucia had climbed yesterday. The feet suddenly disappeared and Haddie's face took its place as well as half her body. She leaned out farther than any sensible person should have. A pair of binoculars hung around her neck and on her head was a black baseball cap turned wrong side round.

"I was beginning to think you'd escaped!" Haddie called down.

"No, we were just messing about on the beach," Max called back.

Max is amazingly literal for a ten-year-old.

There was a pause. Then, "Assuredly you lie! Your pant cuffs aren't damp!" She began reeling in the bicycle from across the moat.

"We rolled them up," Max called back.

"No back talk, thou spleeny canker blossom! You shall all be punished severely! Meet me in the Great Hall. It's the second room on the right up the first passage." Then she hopped on the bicycle and flew across the moat and into her bedroom window.

The severe punishment was a repulsive concoction of peanut butter and marshmallow cream in a sandwich, set out on a slabby wooden table with benches beside it.

"Try it, you'll hate it," Haddie said.

They did, and they did. But they ate the sandwiches anyway, because they were all starving. Max said he liked it, but he was also staring at Haddie in the most ridiculous way so I doubt he was tasting his sandwich at all.

The Great Hall was about the size of a smallish living room, with coffered wood ceilings that were carved with scenes of knights on horseback fighting dragons and knights on horseback fighting each other and occasionally a knight lying dead on the ground with a sword sticking out of his suit of armour. The walls were full of mouldy mounted deer heads, and above a huge grandfather clock was a collection of engraved archery bows. Hanging all around the edges of the room were banners decorated with educational information, like the periodic chart of the elements and place value mathematical charts, and a plant classification chart with mosses, ferns, and angiosperms. The Hardscrabbles imagined that the parents of the Dusty Old Children (that is what the Hardscrabbles began to call the Kneebone children, who did seem like long-gone relics) must have thought they were being very crafty, and I'm sure the Dusty Old Children resented it thoroughly. Even now, the room had a dreary, deserted feel to it—the sort of room that you peer into on the way to somewhere else.

"Have you been in that tower all day?" Lucia asked Haddie, her voice sounding gaggish from the peanut-marshmallow sludge that was clinging to the roof of her mouth.

"If I say yes, will you want to know why?" Haddie replied.

"Probably."

Haddie lifted the baseball cap off her head. There was a pink impression low on her forehead where the cap's adjustable strap had bit into her skin. She slapped the cap back on her head, bill forward, and rubbed her knuckles across the bottom of her chin, considering things.

"What do people *usually* do in a siege tower?" Haddie said finally.

"They watch the enemy for signs of weakness as the army prepares to storm the castle." Max answered this so promptly it was as though he'd been waiting forever for someone to ask that very question.

"Give that man a Pixy Stix," Haddie said.

"A what?" Lucia asked.

"Hold on." She left then returned a moment later with a handful of colorful straws, one of which she threw at Max like a dart. He caught it in midair. That impressed Haddie and she tossed him another, just to see if he could do it again. He fumbled that one.

"So are you going to storm Kneebone Castle?" Lucia asked.

"Me? Oh, no. I'm just the brains of this operation. I'll have my brave knights storm the castle for me."

"But you don't have any brave knights," Max pointed out.

"A small glitch. Not to worry," Haddie replied.

"So who's the enemy?" Lucia asked as Max tore open one end of the straw, poured a blue powder in his hand, and smelled it. Chester walked across the table to sniff at it too, took a small lick, and sneezed.

"The enemy lives in Kneebone Castle, of course," Haddie said, her voice taking on the tongue-rolling ye-and-thee-and-thou tone. "The scurvy fiend shall feel the wind of my arrows graze his cheek before the moon wanes full."

"The moon *waxes* full," Max corrected.

"Wanes."

"Waxes."

"Do you know what happened to Galileo when he said that the earth rotates around the sun?" Haddie asked him sternly.

"He was put under house arrest for the rest of his life," Max said with perfect certainty.

"Really?" Haddie raised her eyebrows. "I just thought no one ever talked to him again."

"What did he do to you? The enemy, I mean," Lucia asked.

Haddie eyed her warily. She popped the last bit of sandwich in her mouth, then scraped a glob of marshmallow cream off her thumb with her teeth. "I'll tell you when I know you better."

"But we'll only be here for a few days," Lucia protested.

"I'm a fast learner," Haddie said.

"Was it really dreadful?" Lucia pursued. She sniffed out a noble quest, with revenge at the center, and that was a subject worth pursuing.

"Let's put it this way," said Haddie. "I left an air-conditioned apartment on the Upper East Side of Manhattan with a take-out Japanese noodle shop on the corner to come to Snoring-by-the-Sea for the summer." Haddie looked around at the Hardscrabbles who were staring blankly at her. *"So, yes, it was really dreadful."*

And her face was now pinched into an expression that left them in no doubt that it really was.

Max finished licking the blue stuff off his hand. He stared at the blue stain on his palm for a minute and then said, "Lucia thinks our mum is dead. I say she's not." He looked up at Haddie. "Who do you say is right?"

For an instant Haddie looked gravely alarmed. It was just an instant before the look vanished.

"What does your father say?" she asked, her voice pointedly nonchalant.

"He says she's gone missing," Max told her. "He says he's quite sure we'll find her someday, but in the meantime we need to carry on with our lives."

"Carry on with your lives? Oh, good one, Casper!" Haddie snorted, then said, "Sorry. That just popped out."

"Well, I think he's right," Lucia said staunchly. "We *should* carry on with our lives."

"Of course you should," Haddie said without any sincerity at all.

"Were you very close with her? What was she like?" Max asked Haddie. His voice was so keen it was nearly breathless.

"Tess and I . . ." Haddie took a deep breath and let it out. "We were like sisters." She said no more, lost in her own thoughts. But then she realized that all the Hardscrabbles were staring at her, eagerly waiting, so she told them this:

"We lived down the road from each other, you know, back in the States, when we were kids. Tess was three years older but she was an only child so she settled for hanging around with me. She was . . ." She shook her head and her eyes drifted to the corner of the room, just as though Tess Hardscrabble were standing there listening.

"Wherever Tess was, something interesting would happen. I think it was because she wasn't afraid of anything, so the World just said, 'All right, kid, what do you think of this?' and 'Well, if that was fun, how about *this*?' Just like it was trying to impress her.

"The two of us used to talk all the time about what we were going to do with our lives. We had so many plans! We were going to explore live volcanoes and train elephants in Indonesia and live with the Inuit for a year and eat whale blubber, and oh, I can't remember all the things we were going to do. People should have all their big adventures while they're still under the age of fourteen. If you don't, you start to lose your passion for big adventures. It just begins to fade away bit by bit and then you forget you ever wanted adventures in the first place . . . it's criminal the way that happens." She tore open a Pixy Stix and poured the green powder onto her plate, then drew in it with her pinky. The Hardscrabbles watched snakes and dancing figures and elephants appear on the plate.

"Then, one summer," Haddie said, "Tess moved to England with her parents and everything interesting in the World went with her. I saw her years later, but by then it was too late. She was already . . ." Haddie studied the pictures on the plate.

"Already what?" Max asked.

Lucia could have kicked him. If he had just stayed quiet, Lucia was certain that Haddie would have kept on talking. Instead Haddie looked up at them, her eyes finally stopping on Otto.

"Well, *you* must remember your mother, Otto," Haddie said. "You were old enough."

Lucia and Max turned to Otto. He glared at Haddie and then lowered his chin, as though he were suddenly walking into a strong wind. Lucia watched his hands to see what he would say, but he had tucked them beneath his scarf.

"He doesn't remember her at all," Lucia finally answered for him.

"Really? How weird," Haddie said, still watching Otto with interest. "Are you sure she's not lurking somewhere"—Haddie reached across the table and touched the middle of Otto's forehead with her finger—"somewhere in there?"

Otto drew back sharply.

"Well, enough lollygagging." Haddie stood up and turned her baseball cap wrong side round again. "Off with ye! Go search for the secret passageway, like normal kids."

"Is there really one?" Lucia asked.

"It said so in the ad, but I suspect they were lying. I haven't been able to find it. If you can't find it either, it will officially be a scam and I can ask for a partial refund. So don't search too hard." She stood up and tossed the rest of the Pixy Stix to Max. "I'm off to the siege tower again. If you chew on it, you'll get a sugar clog." This last part was said to Max, who was watching Haddie strangely again while chewing on the end of the Pixy Stix contemplatively.

"She's off her trolley," Otto said when she was gone.

"Maybe," Max said, working a clog of coagulated sugar

out of the Pixy Stix. "But haven't you noticed something else about her?"

And then they were right back at the conversation they'd started in the dungeon and had never finished.

"What?" Lucia asked.

Max tapped the Pixy Stix against his hand. "Well . . . haven't you noticed that she looks an awful lot like someone?"

"Tell us already!" Lucia grabbed the Pixy Stix out of his hand.

"Haven't you noticed that she looks exactly like Otto?" Max said, grabbing the Pixy Stix back.

Once it was said, Lucia realized that it was perfectly true. Looking at Otto, Lucia instantly saw the lines of Haddie's face sketched within his own. The pointed cheekbones, the wide upper lip that was thicker than the lower, the high forehead.

"How funny," she murmured.

Otto, however, did not find it funny. Not at all. Even Chester raised his head as though he could feel a tensing-up in Otto's muscles.

"So we look alike," Otto said. "She *is* our aunt, after all."

"Great-aunt," Max corrected. "If you believe her story."

"You don't?" Lucia asked him, surprised.

"No."

There was a space of silence.

"Who is she then?" Lucia asked.

"I'm not sure," Max said. "But I think she may be Mum."

It was amazing how a person who was so clever about most things could also be so silly about others, thought Lucia. She looked at Otto and rolled her eyes, then waited for him to roll his back at her. But he didn't.

Lucia turned back to Max and said, "Why would she call herself Haddie Piggit instead of Tess Hardscrabble then?"

"Haddie Piggit *is* Mum's name," Max said. "Theresa Haddie Piggit-Campbell. Tess for short, Haddie for middle and Piggit-Campbell is her maiden name. It says so right on our birth certificates."

"Haddie is probably a family name," Otto said.

"And anyway, why would she have signed the letter to Dad 'your loving aunt-in-law, Haddie Piggit'?" Lucia asked.

"Maybe it was a code. In case one of us saw the letter. Maybe she's been writing to him all along, for years and years."

"Ridiculous!" Otto said so vehemently that he startled Chester, who jumped out of his arms.

"It is, you know," Lucia said. "Ridiculous, I mean. Mum is gone, Max. Gone as in dead, most likely. She's not coming back. I don't know why you can't accept that. *We* do." She looked over to Otto for agreement but he wasn't looking at her.

"How did Haddie introduce herself to you?" Max asked Lucia suddenly.

"I don't remember. Why?" Lucia replied.

"Think," Max urged.

So she did. So much had happened yesterday that it

was hard to pull out one piece and remember it exactly. She thought back to the conversation she'd had in Haddie's bedroom.

"She didn't introduce herself," Lucia said finally. "I asked her if she were Great-aunt Haddie and she said she was."

"There!" Max jabbed a triumphant finger at her.

"There, what?"

"You told her who you thought she was, and she just agreed," Max explained.

"Maybe she's a total stranger then," Otto suggested.

That sent a little chill through them until Lucia remembered:

"No, she knew my name without my telling her. She even pronounced it right. And she knew which one of you was which."

"She's not Mum!" Otto said, his hands moving angrily. He grabbed Chester up off the floor and stalked out of the room.

They were quiet for a moment out of pure astonishment.

"Why is he so angry?" Max asked.

"It's hard to explain," Lucia said.

And it was. Very. Because she had no idea.

Chapter 11

In which there are no vampires or ghosts
but you'll like this chapter anyway

They found Otto sitting on his bed in the dungeon. Chester was curled in Otto's lap, but Otto wouldn't pet him. He wouldn't get up either, not even when Lucia and Max said they were going to explore the castle folly for the secret passageway. Not even when Lucia demanded that he get up.

This annoyed Lucia greatly. "Fine! Stay here and act like a giant dope," she said.

But Max sat down on the bed beside him, which made the rat come out of the ceiling and scuttle across the floor. Chester looked at it but didn't even bother to get up. You can fool a cat only so many times.

"Come on, old man," Max said gently, putting his arm around Otto. "We'll do some exploring and maybe find something for your collection. There's bound to be some weird bugs or something like that."

But Otto wouldn't even look at Max. He raised his knees so fast that Chester tumbled out of his lap. He crossed his arms on top of his knees and laid the side of his face against his arm. There he sat, in a gloomy funk, and he looked so much like a real prisoner in a real dungeon waiting for his execution that Lucia laughed, which was probably wrong of her. In any case, it didn't help matters. He wouldn't budge.

In the end, Lucia and Max went exploring without him. They travelled through hallways that twisted and turned and made them fear they were hopelessly lost until they realized they had passed the same big china jug that was used as an umbrella stand five times. They tried every stairway. One whirled tightly, up and up, until they were sure it would lead them to one of the towers, only to find that the stairwell ended disappointingly at a stone wall. Other stairwells opened into small, strangely shaped rooms—octagonal or hexagonal—with moth-eaten tapestries on the walls and wormy wooden cupboards whose drawers contained exactly nothing at all, except for a bee spray in one. Max and Lucia used the spray can to tap at the walls, listening for the hollow sound of a secret passageway. All the while they looked, they thought about Haddie and about their mum, and wondered.

"The thing is, if it really is *her*," Lucia said suddenly, "why wouldn't she just say so?"

"She may be afraid to," Max answered very promptly, because he'd been thinking the same thing.

"Afraid of *us*?" Lucia said doubtfully.

"Afraid what we'll think of her," Max said.

That brought up a very important point. What *should* they think of a mum who has left her kids? The question made Lucia feel very squirmish in her gut. It was one thing to assume that your mum had met some tragic end. It was quite another to think that she had simply packed up her things and left you deliberately.

"Well, anyway, Otto says it's not her." Lucia tried to sound decided.

"How would he know when he doesn't even remember her?" Max replied.

"Maybe not consciously, but he'd know. Deep down."

She thought that would put an end to the whole thing. Of course it didn't, as you'll see, but it made her feel much better, and she began to search the rooms with more gusto.

Finally, they did manage to find something remarkable. Tucked away in one of the towers was a small round room with a little carousel in the center. The beautifully painted wooden horses were clad in armour, like knights' steeds. The lip of the platform and roof were carved with tangles of leaves and flowers, painted gold, and in the center of the carousel was a painting of a smiling king and queen and three haughty-looking princesses.

"Does it work, do you think?" Lucia asked Max.

Max walked around the carousel until he found a lever,

which he yanked up. Immediately, the carousel began to move and the room was filled with plinky carousel music. Lucia and Max wasted no time in hopping up on the platform and each mounted a horse. Of course, carousels are completely for infants, but if you had discovered one unexpectedly and you didn't have to pay for a ticket, you would have ridden it too, you know you would.

They rode until they had circled the royal family a dozen times or so, and then they grew completely bored.

"I can't imagine that the Dusty Old Children used this thing too much," Max said as he and Lucia dismounted, then made wobbly leaps off the platform before pulling down the lever.

"No, I think it's one of those things that seems like a good idea before you actually have it," Lucia agreed.

They continued their search, coming to a cozy, dark-paneled library. There was a small marble fireplace and squat, tooled-leather chairs, and a spinning globe. The shelves were full of children's books—some of which they'd heard of but most they had not—and a child-size ladder rolled around the edge of the shelves. They took turns pushing each other around the room on the ladder, spun the globe for a while, and then, just to be thorough, checked behind a tapestry on the wall for a secret passageway.

They found something.

It wasn't a secret passageway. It was a small alcove, and on the floor was a hole with a flat brass ring circling it. Engraved in the brass was this poem:

IF THERE'S SOMETHING YOU WANT TO LOSE
BROCCOLI, SMASHED VASE, UGLY SHOES
DROP IT HERE IN THE ABYSS
THE ONLY RULE IS PLEASE NO PISS

Lucia dug in her pocket and pulled out ten pence and dropped it in. She listened for a *plunk* but it never came.

"Well, that was waste of money," Max said. He knelt by the hole and put his eye to it. "I can't see the bottom."

"Hence, the Abyss," Lucia said.

"Hang on. I see something." He adjusted his body so that he lay flat on his right side and shoved his arm down the hole. After a moment of pawing around, he sat up grasping a stick.

"A stick. Oh, well done, Max," Lucia said.

"It's not a stick," Max said. "It's an arrow."

Indeed, on closer inspection it was an arrow. Its shaft was green and it had grimy white feather fletches bound to the end.

"The tip was wedged in the side of the hole," Max said, wiping dirt off of it. The tip was gold colored and was all jaggedy along one edge as though someone had bitten it.

"Weird-looking thing," Lucia said.

"Otto might like to see it," Max said.

"I'm sure he would," Lucia readily agreed.

So they decided to head straight back to the dungeon. They were tired of exploring, and truth be told, they had an idea that their explorations were doomed to failure because Otto wasn't with them. He knew how to find hidden things,

140

whereas Max and Lucia did not. He would have no doubt led them to the secret passageway without any trouble.

Finding their way back to the dungeon wasn't easy. The stairwells tricked them again and again, some of them ending in walls at the bottom, some of them twisting about so that suddenly they were going up again. It was pretty maddening. Finally, they went down a stairwell that led them straight into a small foyer. At the end of the foyer was a low wooden door.

"Probably a broom closet." Max sighed.

But when they opened the door they found that it led directly outside, into the grassy courtyard. It wasn't where they wanted to go, but they were grateful for the rush of fresh air. They both collapsed on the grass and let the cool sea breeze dry the sweat on their faces. It was very pleasant, and Lucia considered that she and Max had spent more time alone together that day than they had in ages, playing in the sea and exploring the castle folly, and that it had been rather fun.

She cleared her throat. "You're not at all bad company," she told him.

"I don't mind you either," he replied.

That was very sentimental for them, you understand. It changed things too. They still fought afterwards, of course, but things never got quite as ugly as they had before.

"What say you, prisoners? Can I ask for a partial refund?" Haddie was standing just behind them, a large purple rucksack hung over one shoulder, limp with emptiness.

"We didn't find anything, but Otto hasn't had a go yet," Max said.

"Tell him not to strain himself." She yanked the slipping rucksack straps back on her shoulder. "Well, I'm off to the post office."

"You must get an awful lot of letters," Lucia said, eyeing the rucksack. All the while a small voice in Lucia's head murmured, *Are you Mum? Could you be? No, not possible. Are you Mum?*

"Letters? Pfff! I go there for my groceries. Nibblies Imports of London sends me a shipment every week. *American* food. Fluffernutter, Twinkies, root beer, Pixy Stix, Hershey's Kisses. How else would I survive in this wilderness? Well, behave yourselves. And whatever you do, stay off of the siege tower."

They climbed the siege tower as soon as Haddie was out of sight.

In broad daylight, the climb up the tower was much more frightening than it had been at night. Now you could see the ground below, which was very far down indeed. Lucia went first, with Max right behind her. Several times she stopped during the ascent to collect her nerves. Each time Max would make some comment like, "The view to the sea is perfect right here" or "You can see clear over the treetops, can't you?" as though Lucia was stopping to sightsee. Maybe he thought she was, or maybe he was just being polite. Either way, she was grateful.

Finally, they reached the top of the tower and stepped onto the platform. Haddie's binoculars lay on a shallow shelf just below the tower's east-facing side, the side that looked out onto Kneebone Castle.

They had a brief struggle over the binoculars.

"What are those lumpy things in the courtyard?" Lucia asked.

"Urns," Max said, staring through the binoculars (Lucia hadn't put her whole into the struggle for them, since Max hadn't been a complete prat about the climb).

"But do you see anybody?" Lucia asked impatiently.

"Nobody. The courtyard is empty. Wait! What's that?"

"What?" Lucia pressed her head against Max's as though she could see what he was seeing that way.

"Never mind. It's just a statue," Max said.

"Oh, for heaven's sake!" Lucia grabbed the binoculars out of Max's hands and looked through them. The courtyard was indeed empty. Although the castle folly was a duplicate of the Kneebone Castle, the two courtyards couldn't have been more different. The grand castle's courtyard was spare and uninviting, with not a single flower or hedge. There were several stone urns with no plants in them and there were statues scattered about, in the form of dancing naked women and fat babies playing instruments. Lucia thought that they looked rather pathetic, the way their music teacher Mrs. Blixton looked when she pranced around clapping her hands, in an attempt to get the class excited about music. The front door was like the castle folly's, only much larger, and was enclosed by a sort of cage made of wrought iron.

Max had been right. It didn't look as though the owners

of the Kneebone Castle were interested in having any visitors.

Lucia moved the binoculars up to scan the castle windows. Many of them were covered with curtains. The windows she could see into showed dark interiors, walls covered with wainscoting and, here and there, pieces of heavy furniture. In one window she could see a desk with piles of paper covering it. Sitting behind the desk, his back to the window and his head bent over the papers, was a black-haired man. Every so often the man leaned back in his chair and scratched at his head furiously, then bent his head over the papers once again.

"Anything interesting?" Max asked.

"Not really."

She tipped the binoculars up and caught sight of a person walking past one window—too fast to see anything—then through another window was a woman carrying a tray. That window must have been in a staircase because she was moving upwards. Lucia could see the top of her body, then her hands carrying a tray with a plate of food and a cup, then her rump, and finally her feet. She was wearing a uniform of some sort.

"Anything?" Max repeated.

"A maid, I think."

Tipping the binoculars up higher, she scanned more windows. More drawn curtains. A few side turrets with missing slates on their roofs. A crow perched on a window ledge that flew away a second later, as though it knew it was being watched.

Then she spotted it. A figure in the window of the far tower. The angle was too sideways for her to see the person clearly, but she could make out a pale face and a slender body that stood very still. Too still. It gave Lucia an eerie sensation and she felt compelled to watch until the figure moved, just a little. It was like a superstitious sort of thing.

"What is it?" Max asked.

"A person. I think the same person who we saw before. In the tower window."

"Can I see?" he asked.

Lucia hesitated. She didn't want to stop watching until the person moved, but it was too ridiculous to say that to Max, so she reluctantly passed the binoculars to him. He moved the binoculars around to find the window while Lucia looked on. But when the binoculars kept shifting, she asked, "Don't you see it?"

"No."

"Give them here." She took the binoculars back and aimed the lens for the tower window. The person was gone.

This is not a book about ghosts or vampires, but there are stranger things in this world than ghosts and vampires, and Lucia had just seen such a thing, though she didn't know it at the time.

Incidentally, there will be a ghost in this book, but that comes in much later.

Okay, we're almost ready to bring The Kneebone Boy in.

Chapter 12

In which Haddie isn't at all like the Empress Amalie
of Schwartzenstadt-Russeldorf. Then something spooky
happens to Lucia in the woods.

Besides her disgusting American groceries, Haddie brought back some normal food for them—sausages, which they cooked over the Bunsen burner, a can of beans ditto, and a box of Jaffa Cakes. She even bought tins of cat food for Chester. She also bought toothbrushes and handed them a bag of clothes, which was very decent of her though the sizes weren't quite right. There were pyjamas for all of them too, the tops of which showed a picture of a lavender hippo wearing dark sunglasses asleep on the beach with musical notes coming out of its nose. Beneath the picture it said, SNORING BY THE SEA . . . DO NOT DISTURB. The same picture and words were printed on the bum of the pyjama shorts too.

"Don't look at me that way," Haddie said, "it's all they had in the shop."

The fresh underwear was much appreciated.

Haddie made dinner for them but Otto wouldn't come out of the dungeon, not even when they let him have the arrow they'd found in the hole. During supper, Lucia stole careful glances at Haddie. She checked her hands for freckles that right side up looked like a bowler hat and upside down looked like a dog with floppy ears. There were some freckles on her hands but they didn't form any pictures. Still, Lucia supposed she might have been wrong about that particular memory. Haddie's eyes were a different shade of blue than Otto's. More greeny. And her chin was rounder than Otto's. Other than that, Lucia had to admit, they were spitting images of each other.

The funny thing about possibly finding a mother whom you lost many years ago is that you don't necessarily fall into each other's arms with joy. Especially when that possible mother appears to be in no hurry to admit she is your mother. *If* Haddie was their mother, Lucia, for one, would have liked an apology for having run off. A tearful one, preferably.

And another thing, Haddie wasn't at all like the Empress Amalie of Schwartzenstadt-Russeldorf, whom Lucia had secretly imagined her mother to be like. In Casper's sketch, the Empress Amalie was tall and willowy with long, silky, flaxen blond hair and a patient, sweet-tempered face. She was perched on a large rock holding a book while birds and rabbits and hedgehogs played around her. By her feet sat a little girl with blond, curly hair and a cranky face, who was dipping a biscuit into a teacup. The empress looked like the type of person who read books out loud beautifully, which is to say she tapped her *t*'s and hissed her *s*'s and stopped reading at just the right parts.

Haddie, on the other hand, was on the short side, and wiry. She looked like the only girl on the boys' football team. And she didn't appear to have a way with birds and rabbits and hedgehogs. She didn't tap her *t*'s and hiss her *s*'s. In fact she had a raspy voice, like someone who might have spent a large part of her teenage years smoking cigarettes.

Once during dinner, Lucia almost spat out the question: "Well, are you or aren't you our mum?!" But then she felt a flip-floppy feeling in her stomach and she chickened out.

Max, too, seemed in no hurry to ask Haddie outright if she was their mum. Lucia thinks it was because he was petrified that the answer would be no, but Max insists he was waiting for the right moment.

At one point Lucia said, "Haddie," her voice going up on the "die" part of her name as though she was about to ask a question. Max was afraid she was going to ask *the* question and tried to kick her under the table but he hit the table leg instead and spilled everyone's root beer. In the end, all Lucia had wanted to know was if they could use the phone to call Mrs. Carnival, which they had forgotten to do.

They called her after dinner. Lucia did it because Max always told too much when he was nervous. This is how the call went:

Brriiing.

MRS. CARNIVAL: Yes?

LUCIA: Hello, Mrs. Carnival, this is Lucia Hardscrabble and I'm calling just to let—

MRS. CARNIVAL: I'm watching my show. Make it quick.

LUCIA: Well, I was just saying that our father sent us to London to—

MRS. CARNIVAL: So he's come to his senses! Good for him! Well, I've told him again and again that it was the thing to do, at the very least with that older boy. No use burdening himself with a deranged child. But I see he's found a new home for all of you at once. It's for the best, you'll see after a while—

LUCIA: No! We're not—oh, for heaven's sake, if our father calls just tell him that we are at Great-aunt Haddie's in Snoring-by-the-Sea.

Lucia hung up.

Max didn't ask what Mrs. Carnival had said. It was enough to see Lucia's face turn an alarming purple and her black eyebrows press together so hard it was as if they were trying to shove each other off her face.

Down in the dungeon, Otto was sitting in the darkest corner. Chester jumped from his lap and ran to them, mewling in a frantic sort of way. That made Lucia feel awful about having left Otto for the entire afternoon, and she hurried to hand him the plate of food that she'd fixed for him upstairs.

"We need to leave," Otto said, pushing the plate toward

Chester, who after a pause to see if Otto meant it, began to pick at the sausage as daintily as an old lady.

"We will," Lucia said. "In a few days."

"I mean *now*," Otto said.

He was so agitated that it unsettled Lucia. She sat beside him on the floor and said very gently, "It's too dark out, Otto. We'd never find our way back to the station, and the trains won't be running to Little Tunks at this time anyway."

"Tomorrow then," Otto said. "In the morning."

"But we don't have money for train tickets," Max said, very reasonably.

"We'll ring Mrs. Carnival. She'll fetch us."

"But why?" Max said, his voice rising with agitation because he knew she would come fetch them, pronto. "*Why* do you want to leave?"

"I don't like her," Otto said, tugging at his hair.

"Haddie you mean?" Max said. "But she's perfectly brilliant."

"Well, I don't trust her."

"Why? What on earth has she done to you?" Max asked.

"I don't like the way she looks at me," Otto muttered.

Max rolled his eyes.

"She looks at me like she knows something about me," Otto said. "And it's none of her business."

"She looks at all of us that way," Max said falteringly. He was faltering because it was a lie and he was an awful liar and they all knew he was lying, so he shouted, "I'm not going back to Little Tunks! She might very well be Mum, and if she is I want to be with her, even if it's just for a couple of days. And if she's not, well, I would still rather be with her a million times more than with Mrs. Carnival!"

"Stay then," Otto said. "But *we* won't." He turned to Lucia for confirmation.

Many thoughts flashed through Lucia's mind just then. She thought about Kneebone Castle and the person in the window. She thought of the wild, churning sea at the bottom of the cliff and the exotic, faraway smell that wafted up from it. And she thought of Haddie, who might be their mother, but even if she wasn't, she had *known* their mother. Had said that Mum was a peach.

"I want to stay too," Lucia said. "I'm sorry, Otto."

Otto looked at her in shocked disbelief. Lucia always stuck by him, with Max on the outside. The pained expression on Otto's face made Lucia's heart ache and she wished she could change her mind, she really did, but the thing of it was, life had suddenly become extraordinarily interesting and who knew when that would happen again? It certainly wouldn't happen back in Little Tunks.

There was nothing left to say to one another, and they were frankly tired out from a very long, eventful day, so they all went to bed early.

Lucia meant to make things up to Otto. She would stay by his side the whole time they were at Haddie's, even when he was sulky. She meant to do all sorts of nice things for Otto, but when morning came she saw that she'd never get the chance to. His bed was empty.

"Max!" Lucia jumped out of bed and pushed at Max's ribs while the rat skittered across the floor. "Get up, get up, Otto's gone!"

He woke, but slowly, and this was no time for slowness.

"Get up, come on!" Lucia began to yank on her clothes hurriedly. "We've got to catch him."

"Catch him doing what?" Max asked groggily.

"Going back home, of course." She felt dizzy and sick, but that might have had something to do with flinging herself out of bed so fast.

"He can't go back home. He won't be able to talk to Mrs. Carnival on the phone, and he hasn't got a ticket, has he?" Max said while easing himself out of bed.

"He has enough money to buy one ticket for himself, though. I thought about it last night and he does. But he can't go home by himself! It's ridiculous! He won't be able to manage . . ." She was about to say "without me" but that sounded too conceited, although it was perfectly true. "Hurry, hurry, will you?" She shoved her feet into her trainers.

When Max was dressed, Lucia rushed upstairs and out into the courtyard, with Max running behind her. The fog was so dense that she found her way to the gatehouse only through sheer luck, colliding once, but painfully, with the curtain wall. The thought of Otto wandering by himself in this fog, lost somewhere in the countryside, made her feel lightheaded with panic. She ran faster, across the drawbridge and out into the meadow through the soppy grass. She turned quickly to check that Max was still behind her.

He wasn't.

"Max! *Max?!*"

She paused to listen but there was no answer. The world was lost in a smoky white fog. Off to her right she could hear the ocean slapping against the cliffs. She turned her back to it and gazed blindly into the distance. If she squinted, she could just make out a rise of a gauzy green. Remembering the funeral carriage's speedy descent down the wooded lane and into valley, she guessed that might be the way back to town.

She called for Max a few more times, but when there was no answer, she headed stalwartly for the green hill in the distance.

It wasn't long before she seriously regretted having rushed off without Max. His sense of direction was far better than hers, and besides, she wanted his company. Every so often she paused to call for him, and once she thought she heard a voice calling back, though it didn't sound quite like his, and when she called to it again there was only silence.

The going was slow. She pressed through the fog carefully, keeping her eyes fixed on the hill. This must be how it is when you are at sea and aiming for land in the far distance, she thought. That took her mind off the more troubling things. She imagined that she was sailing through the West Indies in the midst of a sudden squall. The rain was blinding and the wild waves were tossing the ship dangerously. She could smell the tarred ropes and could hear the sailors rushing about, trying to mend a torn mizzen mast. A sudden pitch and she nearly tumbled into the violent sea (she had just stumbled on a rock on the path), but her lieutenant caught her greatcoat just in time and pulled her back in. No, she didn't like that. She thought she ought to be the one who saved her lieutenant instead. So she did, and by the time he had thanked her profusely for saving his life, and she had managed to steer the ship through the eye of the storm, the fog started to lift.

The thick whiteness grew wispier by the minute as Lucia ascended the hill. The wooded lane looked very similar to the one they travelled through in the funeral carriage, although much less forbidding in the daylight. In fact, it was quite a beautiful lane, flanked by quiet old trees and sprays of wildflowers. It was wonderfully peaceful. But in books the worst things happen to people when they are feeling very relaxed, so Lucia was vigilant as she walked.

Every so often she called out, "Otto!" and sometimes, "Max?"

It was when she was nearly at the top of a particularly steep incline that she heard it. It sounded like fingernail frantically scratching at a mosquito bite under the heel of a cotton sock.

She stopped short, her eyes wide. The scratching sound had ceased. It might be Otto, she thought very reasonably, though her heart was pounding beneath her ribs. He couldn't call back, and in any case he was so angry that he wouldn't come to her.

A snap of a branch made her jump. A more unreasonable thought entered her brain—that someone other than Otto was lurking in the woods; that the person was watching her even now. She listened hard but could hear nothing more than the sound of leaves rustling as birds darted from tree to tree, and the deep silence of the wood. The woods seemed to be listening to her too. She forced herself to keep moving, and then began to listen to herself as well. Her footsteps were heavy and she could hear the rhythm of fear in them. Was it fear for herself or for Otto? Both probably, she thought, but in either case she didn't like it. It struck her as cowardice. She willed her feet to land more lightly, pressing her heels down firmly with each step and rolling onto her toes. Still she couldn't shake the feeling that she wasn't alone. It came from reading too many novels, she told herself. From now on, she vowed, she would read more nonfiction, like Max.

"Max, Max, where are you?" Lucia murmured under her breath. It surprised her how much she wanted him with her now. He would have been quite logical about the whole thing. His perspective would have been friendlier as well. She tried to imagine what he would say: "Why shouldn't someone else be walking through the woods? They might be on their way to the beach or enjoying the wildflowers. Or maybe it's just Haddie, out for a stroll."

That was when she saw it—a human shape standing

between two silver birch trees. As soon as she noticed it, it darted away and then disappeared into the shadows. Lucia froze, her eyes scanning the woods, listening. All was quiet. Even the birdsong had ceased.

Was the figure male or female? Dark haired or light? Lucia couldn't tell. The person had moved too quickly and stayed in the shadows, as though he or she knew how to conceal him- or herself in the woods.

Every cell in her body urged her to flee. The muscles in her legs were clenched tight, ready to spring off down the footpath. But Lucia's pride was deep, and she hated to think of someone getting the better of her.

"Who are you?" she called into the woods.

There was no answer. She wondered if someone was trying to frighten her.

"I know you're there!" she called out again. "You might as well come out and show yourself!"

She paused, listened. There was silence, as though the person was considering what to do next. But after several minutes, when no one emerged and no further sound was made, Lucia wondered if the person was far away by now. She even began to doubt what she had seen. Maybe the figure was only a rogue shadow thrown from the shifting canopy of leaves. She pulled in a long, deep breath to still the quivery feeling in her legs. For good measure, she called out, "You're not that clever! I can see you perfectly well!"

"Well, you'd have to be bloody blind not to," growled a voice. She whipped around to find Saint George directly behind her on the footpath. He wore a khaki green shirt and khaki green trousers, snug below the knee, due apparently to a pair of calves the size of prize-winning yams. Also, and most importantly, he had a rifle leaning against his shoulder.

Chapter 13

In which we finally meet
The Kneebone Boy. Sort of.

"Was that you?" Lucia asked breathlessly. "Back there? Dashing about?"

"I don't *dash*," he said. There was a quiet, sneering tone to his voice. If he had been dressed well, Lucia would have thought he was a terrible snob.

"I suppose you're planning on shooting little bunnies," Lucia said, trying hard to adopt a similar air of disdain and recover some of the dignity that she'd lost a moment ago.

"It's none of your damn business what I'm doing," he said, glowering at her. But then he seemed to reconsider her, and he added, "Anyway, I'm looking out for rarer game than bunnies. It's curiosities that pay the bills. Now tell me, what was it you saw *dashing* about the woods?" he asked.

Lucia suddenly felt a peculiar resistance to talking about that shadowy figure. "I don't know. Nothing. It was probably just an animal. What is the curiosity you're hunting?"

Saint George sniffed, his lower lip pushing at his upper lip so that it nearly touched his nostrils. Lucia had the uncomfortable sensation that he was picking up her scent, the way a lion picks up the scent of a nervous zebra. Or of a white pony soon to be painted with black stripes. He gazed down at her importantly, and for the thousandth time in her life, Lucia wished that she were taller.

"Ever heard of The Kneebone Boy?" he asked.

Lucia shook her head.

"Well, he's the one I'm after. He's shifty, no doubt, but I'm on that boy's scent. It won't be long."

"A boy!" Lucia cried, appalled. "You're hunting a boy?"

"Maybe he's a boy and maybe he isn't." Saint George glanced down at Lucia slyly. "Some say he's part animal, covered with hair, with claws for hands and ears like a bat's. When his mother first laid eyes on him she fainted dead away, and his father had him shut up in a tower room at Kneebone Castle, out of people's sight. Still, for hundreds of years, people have been hearing wailing and screaming through the castle walls."

"Hundreds of years?" Lucia snorted. Although she often read books about the supernatural, she was not so silly as to believe in it. "Are you saying that The Kneebone Boy is hundreds of years old?"

"Not that very one, no. There's been generations of

them since that first one. It seems that in the Kneebone family, the firstborn sons always have something horribly wrong with them."

"Like bat's ears and claws?" Lucia said scornfully.

"Yeah, well . . . I didn't say I believed that rot. Me, I guess it's probably just some sort of deformity, something bad enough for the family to want to hide. Now he's managed to escape from the tower room again, hasn't he? He does from time to time and then they catch him and shut him up again, poor sod. He's close by, though. I spied him back there just a bit ago."

"Are you going to shoot him?" Lucia cried in horror.

"Shoot him? Of course not. What good would that do me? I'm going to catch him. Catch him and keep him for a bit. There's a lot of gossip rags that'd pay sweet for a picture of The Kneebone Boy in the flesh. I don't know what the going price is on a legend, but I imagine it's a sight better than the price of a stuffed hedgehog."

"Yes, I imagine," Lucia agreed, nodding thoughtfully.

You might be surprised that she didn't call him all sorts of names. But just wait, you'll understand in a minute.

"How are you going to catch him then?" Lucia asked, in a pleasant and interested tone.

"Traps," Saint George said proudly. "I've set dozens of them all through the woods. Just been to check on them now."

"Traps! That's clever. What sort of traps are they?" she asked. (Do you see now?)

"The sort that will catch a boy. Would you like me to show you where I've put them?" Saint George offered.

"Oh, yes," Lucia said.

Saint George let out a nasty, barking laugh. "Oh, yes, I'm sure you would. Do you honestly think I'm that daft?"

Lucia turned bright red because she hated to be laughed at, especially when she thought she was being so shrewd.

"Yes, I do think you're that daft!" she cried out at him. "And unethical! And absolutely repulsive!"

She stormed off then, no longer afraid to be in the woods alone. If it was The Kneebone Boy who was lurking, she'd rather run into him than be in the company of Saint George for a moment longer.

"Take the right-hand turn if you want to get to town!" Saint George called after. "If you go left, you'll wind up at Wigbottom's place, and Mrs. Wigbottom will feed you canned peaches and talk your ear off about the . . ." He was far behind her at this point, so his last word was not very clear but she thought he said "ruddy winnies." It might have been the "ruddy windies." In either case it didn't make any sense. She could still hear the laughter in his voice, so that when she did come to the fork in the path, she very nearly took the left turn. But she could see that the woods began to thin along the right-hand path, and it seemed foolish to go the wrong way just on principle.

A few minutes later, she found herself on an open country lane. She hurried past a stone farmhouse with a vast, mucky pasture speckled with cattle. The animals lifted their heads lazily to stare at her as she passed. It reminded her of the way some of the bolder kids in Little Tunks stared at Otto before she taught them not to, with her fists.

Off in the distance she heard a rumble. It was so faint that she thought nothing of it, but as she walked the rumble grew louder. She glanced over the stretch of fields to her right, in the direction of the noise. At first she saw nothing. But by the time the lane turned into paved road, and more houses appeared, huddling closer and closer together as the road progressed, Lucia heard a whistle and saw flashes of metal in the distance, appearing between the trees. The train!

She began to run now, knowing full well that it was an impossible race. Yet it was the only thing she could think to do. The train was roaring through the town so loudly that she could barely hear her own shoes as they pounded on the pavement.

She spotted Saint George's shop, noting the CLOSED sign out front, and sneered even as she ran past. Still, her mind was so full of Otto there was hardly room in it to hate Saint George properly.

In the heart of town, she passed several people who stared at her suspiciously as she darted by. This was the sort of town, like Little Tunks, where a kid couldn't run without someone wondering if she'd just pinched something at the store.

The train's roar subsided then stopped altogether. Otto would be boarding the train now. Without her. She kept up her pace anyway, even though the station was still far off, too far for her to make it in time. Her legs were aching and her breath came in wobbly gasps, the sound of which made her feel more desperate. Why desperate? you are probably thinking. But you have never been the sister to a brother who is very odd and unpredictable. And you have never been the sort of sister who has rarely been more than a few rooms apart from her odd brother, and is not sure what would happen to either of them if they ever were.

By the time Lucia reached the station, the tail of the train was winding around the curve on the track. At the far end of the platform a man in a brown suit and carrying a briefcase walked past the station building and down the steps, but apart from that the platform was empty. Lucia stared after the train despairingly, watching it whip around the final bend and disappear from view.

Did all grand adventures go so utterly wrong? Sometimes they did in books, but in real life they feel far worse. In real life you can't put the book down and collect yourself with a piece of charred toast and butter. You have to keep on feeling bad, and hungry too, if you haven't had any breakfast, which Lucia had not.

She stood there for a moment, her breath still drawing in hard, shivery gulps from her run. Out of the corner of her eye, from behind the brick station building, she saw a slender black ribbon twitch in the breezeless air then disappear as though someone had yanked it back. She stared curiously at the spot where it had been.

A few seconds later a black cat appeared from behind

the building, its tail curled into a question mark and a fifth leg swinging right in front of its hind one. Lucia opened her mouth to call out in joy, then ran instead, laughing while the cat watched, its tail unravelling then re-forming its question mark. Scooping up Chester, Lucia peered around the side of the station building. And there he was! There they *both* were! Otto, sitting on a bench bolted to the building, with a disgruntled look on his face, and Max standing in front of him with his hands tucked into his back pockets.

"You didn't leave! Oh, thank goodness! How did you get here so fast? Saint George is despicable. You'll hate him when I tell you . . ." She spoke to Otto then to Max then to both, all the while clutching Chester to her chest. She was so excited that she squeezed the cat too tightly. It yowled in complaint. Otto rose to snatch him out of Lucia's arms, then collapsed back onto the bench.

"They wouldn't let him on the train without a cat carrier," Max explained.

"Thank you, cat," Lucia said to Chester, smiling.

Otto scowled up at her, and her smile faded.

"If I'd known that was the rule, I would have put him in my shirt when I tried to buy the ticket," he grumbled.

It hurt Lucia that he had wanted to leave so badly; that he felt he could manage the train ride and the strange faces, even Mrs. Carnival, without her with him.

"What took you so long to get here?" asked Max.

"Well, I don't have wings, do I?" she said, preferring to be irritated instead of hurt.

"Neither do I but I've been here a solid twenty minutes ahead of you. You must have taken the wrong path. The castle's gatehouse was facing us when we arrived last night, didn't you notice?"

"Of course," Lucia said (she hadn't).

"Then why didn't you take the path opposite?" Max persisted.

"Because I spotted something more interesting on another path," she said. It was not exactly the truth, but never mind.

"What was it?" Max asked.

"The Kneebone Boy," Lucia said. She waited for Max to ask her to explain.

"There's no such thing," Max said. "The Kneebone Boy is just a fairy tale."

"You've heard of him?" Lucia immediately regretted the shock in her voice.

"Of course. There's a whole section about him in Binwater's *Castle Myths and Legends* and the BBC had a show on monsters of the British Isles last summer. Covered in hair. Bat's ears and claws, locked in a secret room, once ripped out the lungs of a doctor who came to see him. . . ."

Lucia hadn't heard that last part.

"Yes, well, the thing I saw in the woods was real enough," she said. "Saint George saw him too."

And she told her brothers the entire story, winding the whole thing up with a finger jab at Max's face. "So you see, genius, there is such a thing as The Kneebone Boy."

Max told her to take her stupid finger out of his face,

which made her poke it into his forehead. This was headed in a bad direction and things might have gotten ugly if Otto hadn't suddenly said, "Do you think you could find them again?"

"Find what?" Lucia asked, noticing that Otto's one visible eye was looking especially alert.

"The two birch trees. You know, the spot where you saw . . . the boy."

"Yes, I think so," Lucia said slowly. "Why?"

"Well, maybe we could find him." There was a sheepish tone in Otto's voice, which Lucia understood immediately.

"Well, we *must* find him, mustn't we?" Lucia said with sudden energy. "What kind of people would we be if we didn't at least try to warn him about Saint George's traps?"

Max says that Lucia was being shamelessly mercenary here. He says that she *knew* searching for a boy with claws and bat ears and whatnot would be irresistible for Otto; that it would keep his mind off of leaving Snoring-by-the-Sea.

Lucia, however, maintains that sometimes you have to start a thing for all the wrong reasons in order to discover the right ones.

Chapter 14

In which Mr. Pickering tells us a story

So we've come to the part of the book in which the Hardscrabbles begin to be less ordinary and more heroic. I wish it had come sooner, so you didn't see us arguing about stupid things so much. And also because of Mr. Dupuis.

"Two important points, old man," Max said, sitting beside Otto and draping his arm across his shoulder. "Number one, I don't know what it is Lucia and Saint George saw, but I'll guarantee you it wasn't The Kneebone Boy."

"Shut up, why don't you?" Lucia hissed at him.

"And number two," Max went on, ignoring Lucia completely, "whatever it was she saw, is not going to be hanging around, waiting for us to find it."

That was true, actually.

"There must be some way to find him," Lucia said.

They sat on the bench and thought, including Max, who could never resist a good think.

"Do you remember," Max said after a while, "how Prince Andrei tamed his black fox?"

"He set a proper table by its den, didn't he?" Lucia said, trying to remember what their father had told them. "And he ate his meals there."

"Right, and he set a plate for the fox too, filled with chicken eggs. And after a while the fox began to get used to the idea of the prince and they ate all their meals together."

"All right," Otto said.

"All right," Lucia agreed.

Max look alarmed. "I didn't mean to literally *do* it. I only mean that if one *was* going to try to make friends with a wild boy that's how one could do it, but I certainly don't think—"

"There's a corner store down the road. We could buy some food," Otto said, rising from the bench, holding Chester.

"Well, that's a complete waste of money," Max objected.

It was two to one, so Max had to go along with it, though as they walked to the corner store he kept grumbling that the birds in the woods would eat the food in the end, and there goes the last of their money, into bird guts.

Lucia on the other hand was well pleased that Otto was going to spend the last of their money. It meant that there wouldn't be any left to pay for his return ticket to Little Tunks.

Outside the market, Otto tucked Chester under his

shirt, arranging his scarf to hide the bump. They bought a loaf of bread, sliced cheese, a package of chocolate digestive biscuits, four bottles of cola, and four packages of cheese-and-onion crisps.

With a cantankerous look on his face, Max eyed the ten-pound note Otto handed to the clerk. Once they were outside, he grumbled, "Fine. Now let's make a few sandwiches, leave them in the woods, and say good-bye to good money."

"We'll need plates," Otto said. "And a tablecloth."

"That's right," Lucia said, happy at the thought of more money spent. "We'll set a proper table like the prince."

Max groaned.

They found a little shop in town called Pickering's This 'n' That, which sold odds and ends and smelled of the fusty old curtains in the school's assembly hall. It was so cluttered with knickknacks that for a few minutes they assumed they were alone in the shop. Otto let Chester out of his shirt and they all wandered through the narrow aisles, hands behind their backs so as not to break anything, gazing around at the shelves of kitten statuettes and flowered jugs and tiny cannons no bigger than a baby's finger, and salt and pepper shakers and porcupine quills trapped in Lucite disks. They fingered through masses of ancient postcards in which people wrote about their cousin Henry who was down with the flu, and that the weather was unseasonably warm or frightfully damp, which shows that the really interesting letters are always thrown away, like Haddie's to Casper.

"Ah, it's a cat!" a thin voice said. "I thought it might be a small dog at first, and they're not allowed, but a cat . . . a cat knows its way around knickknacks. Did you want something in particular?"

It took some looking round to discover who was talking. Sitting on a battered white armchair in the corner of the room was a man in a white button-down shirt that was yellowed around the collar. He had nice, worried brown eyes, very little hair, and crooked eyeteeth.

"Yes," Lucia said. "We need plates."

"Plates. Well," the man slowly rose from his chair. He wasn't very ancient—maybe in his fifties or so—but he moved carefully, like he was quite elderly. The children assumed he was Mr. Pickering, and in fact he was, so we'll call him by his name now. "I do have a few plates," said Mr. Pickering.

He guided them to the back of the store where there was truly the hugest assortment of plates the Hardscrabbles had ever seen: flowered; gold-rimmed; plates with roosters on them; souvenir plates of the Eiffel Tower; plates with Marilyn Monroe on them; and on and on.

"What sort are you looking for?" Mr. Pickering asked, using his thumb to wipe a bit of dust from the edge of a plate festooned with dancing mushrooms. They thought for a minute.

Otto said, "Something majestic."

"Something majestic," Lucia translated.

"Majestic is off to the right, up above the chubby angels, there you are."

There were plates with the Queen's face on it and a few lovely ones of Princes William and Harry and some of Buckingham Palace and others with the royal crests, which were nice and colorful. But the one that caught their eye showed a lumpy castle on the edge of a cliff.

"That's Kneebone Castle!" Lucia pointed.

"Oh, yes," Mr. Pickering said, "there have been quite a few souvenir plates done of Kneebone Castle. Here's one with the original Lord and Lady Kneebone." He pointed to a pale blue plate with two portraits, each inside little gilded ovals. Lord Kneebone had no chin and Lady Kneebone had two of them.

"This one here is of Kneebone Castle as well, but it's very unusual." He took down a plate and held it out for them to look at more closely. "Do you see the red things hanging from windows?"

The Hardscrabbles nodded.

"They're scarves. Famous incident that happened way back in the late 1800s. I'm assuming you know about The Kneebone Boy?"

It took all their self-control not to make eyes at one another. They simply nodded and tried not to look quite as interested as they felt.

"Well, there had been talk about this monster child for many years. That he'd been locked away in a hidden room in the castle. So some smart fellow who was visiting Lord Kneebone waited for him and his lady to leave the castle and then quickly went from room to room, hanging a red scarf out of every window in the castle. When he stepped outside in the courtyard to examine the windows, he saw exactly what he hoped to see: one of the windows had no scarf hanging from it. He hadn't missed it. Oh, no, he was very thorough. It was simply that the room was tucked away, with a secret entrance that was very hard to discover. Right in there." Mr. Pickering tapped one slender white finger on the plate's scarfless window. "That is where The Kneebone Boy was kept prisoner."

The window was high up on the last tower, closest to the sea. You know the window. You've seen the Hardscrabbles stare into it twice already, once when they were on the way to the beach, and again when Lucia was looking through the binoculars.

"Have you ever seen him?" Lucia asked, trying to keep her voice steady.

"Seen him?" Mr. Pickering looked startled, as though it were a question he'd never expected to be asked, and so had not thought up a sensible-sounding answer. "Not seen him, per se."

"Lucia hasn't seen him per se either," Max said, then instantly looked at Lucia because he knew he shouldn't have said it. But Mr. Pickering didn't seem to notice.

"But *something* happened," Lucia urged him after she had made a face at Max.

"Well, yes, but so long ago, and under such strange circumstances that I can't be sure it was anything at all." Mr. Pickering stopped then and there, and probably would not have gone any further.

But then Otto did something most out of the ordinary

for him. He turned to Mr. Pickering and signed to him very earnestly. Of course Mr. Pickering had no idea what Otto was saying, but he guessed that it was an appeal to hear the story. And Mr. Pickering had enough good sense to know that this was no silly appeal, but that important things were at stake. He glanced at the shop door to see that no one was coming in, then crossed his arms against his narrow chest.

"I never saw him, but . . . my father was an electrician, the only one in Snoring, and the Kneebones hired him to wire the folly for electricity. I was about eleven at the time and my dad took me along on the first day, because I'd always wanted to see inside the folly. No one I knew had ever been in there. The Kneebone children all had tutors, so none of the other kids in Snoring had met them, though we'd see them playing by the sea from time to time. So of course I was eager to go.

"But when we crossed the drawbridge and all three of the Kneebone children met us at the gatehouse, I wondered if I'd made an awful mistake. Three fierce faces— two boys and a girl— staring at us just as though we had invaded their castle, which in a way we had. My father didn't notice. He said, 'Have fun,' or something like that and left me at their mercy.

"They questioned me for a few minutes and they made fun of my teeth. After that they were quite friendly. They showed me all their toys and we shot arrows from the siege tower at my cap, which they had swiped from my head and flung to the courtyard below—the younger boy was the best shot. He skewered my poor cap to bits. We even had a joust on their little ponies. I fell off right away but they played on, charging at one another at top speed, hooting and screaming. They were the most fearless, wild children I'd ever met in my life. I was dizzy with admiration.

"Then they said, 'There's another one of us, you know. Our oldest brother. The Kneebone Boy, people call him.' They had a wicked look in their eyes. That should have tipped me off right then, but I was very curious.

"'Do you want to meet him?' they asked. I nodded, too excited and frightened to even speak.

"'We'll take you to him,' they said, 'but we're going a secret way, so first we have to blindfold you.'

"They tied an old rag over my eyes and led me through the house. We stopped suddenly and in a moment I heard noises—a *tap-tap-tap*ping, then scraping and grunting. After that there was a hiss that seemed to fly over my head and then an awful screech. I thought one of the Kneebones was hurt and I said, 'Are you all right?' but they just told me to 'Shut it.' They made me crouch down and pushed me through a door—my head banged against it as I went through. Then they said I could stand up again. Someone held my hand. I hoped it wasn't the girl because my palm was so sweaty. We walked a long way—downhill it felt like. I could smell damp earth and the air was clammy and cold. I put out my free hand and felt a rock wall. After a while, I began to hear water running somewhere far below and soon after that we stopped.

" 'We've got to cross a bridge here,' the girl said.

"Someone placed my hands on the shoulders of the person in front of me. Someone else put their hands on my hips from behind and we walked like that, very slowly. I knew we'd crossed when one of the boys shoved me up against a wall.

" 'Right, here's the part where you could fall and die,' he said. 'So keep your back to the wall and shuffle along sideways until we tell you otherwise.'

"I shuffled very carefully, my heart beating like mad, careful to keep my spine pressed hard against the wall. We went this way for some time. The water sounded very, very far below and I could smell the emptiness of the air around me. Once I tipped the toe of my shoe forward and found that it touched nothing at all. I was terrified the entire time, right up until when the girl said, 'All right, we can walk normal now.'

"But it wasn't quite normal. We were soon walking up steps that were very tricky. Under my feet, they felt bumpy and lopsided. The person holding my hand—it was the girl, much to my embarrassment—kept having to steady me as I fumbled along, tripping every few minutes. We went up and up and up. I was growing winded, and I could hear from their huffing and puffing that they were as well. Then suddenly we stopped.

"They warned me that if I made a single sound they would leave me there all alone, never to be found again, so you can be sure I was quiet as a tomb. They took off my blindfold. We were standing in a tiny little alcove no bigger than a lift. Apart from the rough-cut stairs that we had just climbed, we were completely surrounded by a solid stone wall. At first I thought it must be some trick and they'd led me all this way for nothing. But then they got down on their knees and began to feel around the wall.

"'Found it,' the girl said, and all together they shoved very hard.

"A section of the wall began to move. It swung open as if it had a hinge, though I couldn't see one, and light began to fill that little alcove. We crawled through the opening, which I soon realized was actually the back of a large fireplace. Once through, I stood up and found myself in a room, clean and bare except for a heavy canvas curtain that stretched from one wall to the other, blocking a section of the room from view.

"I looked around carefully, searching for a misshapen creature that might be crouching behind a chair or in a shadowy corner, but the room seemed perfectly empty of anything alive.

"'Is he here?' I whispered shakily.

"'Shh!' the older boy ordered.

"'Charlie?' the girl called out. 'Charlie, sweetheart, we've come for a visit.'

"From behind the curtains, I heard the most awful noise I'd ever heard in my life. It was an animal sound but no, not quite an animal . . . it was too full of frustration and grief. It was so deeply shocking that I was ashamed to hear it, ashamed and terrified. I told them I wanted to leave, but they wouldn't let me spoil their fun so quickly.

" 'Don't be stupid. He can't get at you. He's tied to his bed,' the older boy told me.

"He dragged me over to the curtain while his sister and brother shoved me from behind.

" 'Say hello to Charlie,' the girl ordered. They all watched me carefully. I said hello to the curtain, very quietly. In an instant there was a terrific wailing and rattling—it was the bed, I guess, as The Kneebone Boy struggled to get free. I leapt backwards, convinced the thing would tear free of his ropes and come at me. I ran to the opening in the fireplace and scrambled through. The kids laughed but they had rushed out through the hole too, nearly as fast as I had.

"Except for the younger boy. He still stood by the fireplace, staring at the curtain.

" 'Let's let him out,' he said. 'Just this once. He's only angry because he's tied up. We could take him out to the woods and let him run about.'

" 'Get out of there, will you!' his brother said and he reached through the opening in the wall and yanked the youngest one's trouser legs till he tripped and nearly cracked his skull against the mantel.

"When we were all on the other side, they pushed the wall back into place and we stood there for a moment, catching our breaths and our wits too.

" '*We're* perfectly normal,' the older boy told me. 'It's just the firstborn son, you know. And he won't live very long, they never do. Sixteen at most. Are you going to tell your friends about this?'

"I wasn't sure if they wanted me to or not. Maybe both.

I said I wouldn't though, and they put the blindfold on me and led me back to the folly, and as you can imagine, I never went back there again."

That was the end of Mr. Pickering's story. The Hard-scrabbles were silent for a few moments, thinking.

"So if The Kneebone Boys die young, that one that you met must be dead by now," Max said.

"Probably."

"There may be a new one, though?" Lucia asked.

"I hope not, but yes, there may be. Poor thing. You know, I never did tell a soul about him. Not until now. It's just that your brother . . ." He looked at Otto, his brown eyes frowning. Mr. Pickering pressed two fingers against his mouth as though to stop himself from saying some-thing. "He seemed to want to know so much," he said after a moment.

Lucia could only guess what Mr. Pickering was going to say. But it was a respectable guess because she had thought that very thing as Mr. Pickering had told the story: that Otto reminded her of The Kneebone Boy. Not on the out-side, obviously, but deep, deep within. A strange boy with-out words.

Chapter 15

*In which the Hardscrabbles wait
for their "black fox," and then discover
that there is not enough time*

The thing about the woods is that unless you are a badger or a sparrow or something critter-ish, it's very hard to say exactly where you spotted something.

"It was here, I think," Lucia had said for the fourth or fifth time, and each time she really meant it. She thought she recognized the two silver birch trees until she found another pair just like them a little farther on. Then another.

Chester's tail also became a source of anxiety. It was questioning every noise, curling up so tightly that the tip formed a circle. Otto made it worse by saying spookily, "There's something here. Chester feels it. I do too."

It made the backs of their necks feel very defenseless. Lucia and Max hurried along, but Otto kept stopping and listening. His slouch straightened out and his chin lifted.

He even pushed his hair back away from his eyes, revealing a forehead that people rarely saw. It was on the high side.

"What? What is it?" Lucia and Max asked nervously each time he stopped. It was never anything they could see though.

It's a funny feeling to be searching for someone and at the same time scared that you will actually find him. Still, Mr. Pickering's story had made the Hardscrabbles even more determined to help The Kneebone Boy.

"Are you *sure* it was here? Lucia, think!" Otto shouted after the sixth time that she was "certain" she'd found the spot.

She knew he was shouting by the way he punched his left thumb knuckle against his solar plexus for "think!"

"I'm positive. This is the place," Lucia said, feeling hurt that he'd yelled at her, and she walked off the path to the twin birch trees with more confidence than she really felt.

They set the tablecloth on the ground, fixed four cheese sandwiches, and placed the sandwiches on the plates (they had purchased the special Kneebone Castle plate for The Kneebone Boy. For themselves, they bought three Christmas plates because they were half price), along with the bags of cheese-and-onion crisps, and several chocolate digestives. The sodas were placed at the corners to hold the cloth down in case of a breeze. Otto rolled up the napkins and tucked them under the edge of the plates. It all looked nice, really.

If I were The Kneebone Boy, Lucia thought, and had

been treated like a mangy dog my whole life, I would feel quite chuffed to have people making such a fuss over me.

They sat on the ground, on the edges of the tablecloth, and listened. The forest, they found, was a very polite place. When the wind made the leaves speak, the birds were silent. When the lark sang, the woodpecker paused to take note. Then the woodpecker *tick-tock*ed and the lark shut up. There were times when the sounds came fast and furious but if you really, really listened, they never interrupted one another.

Max pretended to look bored, but really he was listening for the sound of a fingernail frantically scratching at a mosquito bite under the heel of a cotton sock. Once, a tree branch snapped nearby, but that might have been anything, and a few times they heard scurrying through the underbrush but it came to nothing.

"Maybe it's not the right spot after all," Lucia said.

The next moment, though, Otto began to tap urgently against his ear.

They all kept perfectly still and listened. Well, Chester padded around a bit, his tail still questioning but less rigidly. Otto picked him up and held him in his lap. For some time all they could make out was the distant *beep-beep* of some bird.

Then they heard it. Whispering. It sounded like the breeze passing through the leaves, only there were words in it, though they couldn't make out what the words were. It was so eerie it made the napes of their necks feel all squibbly. Chester too seemed anxious, his ears swivelling this way and that. The children looked up at the shifting canopy of leaves and all around through the shadowy green depths of the woods, but they couldn't see anything that looked like a boy. It was as though the whispering had melted into the air around them.

"Who's there?!" Max shouted, his voice all nerves. It made Otto and Lucia jump. The whispering stopped. Secretly, Lucia was glad but when she looked at Otto, she saw that he was frowning.

"What did you do that for?" Lucia griped at Max, on Otto's behalf. "Now you've scared him off."

"Good! It gave me the shivers," Max said.

"I thought you said The Kneebone Boy was just a myth," Lucia said.

"Well, someone is out there, I don't know who, and I don't like the way they're sneaking about."

They waited a few minutes more, then ate their food and drank their sodas, remembering that it had taken Prince Alexei several tries before the fox came out of his den and joined him for a meal. They left The Kneebone Boy's food for him, just as the prince had left the eggs for his fox, and were about to head back to the folly when Lucia remembered.

"Wait!" she said. "We have to warn him about Saint George. Who has pen and paper?"

No one did.

"Give us those Pixy Stix then." Lucia held her hand out toward Max.

"What Pixy Stix?" Max tried to look honest.

Lucia made a fast lunge at Max and whipped the bundle of colored straws out of his side pocket.

"Oi! That's nerve!" he cried.

But Lucia ignored him. She scoured around until she found a nice, flat rock and she placed it at the base of one of the birch trees. Kneeling in front of it, she carefully wrote a message with the Pixy powder on the rock.

It is very hard to write legibly with colored sugar. She had to do some editing with spit and her forefinger until she was satisfied with the message:

"BEWARE OF TRAPS BY BIG MAN WITH BRAIN," Max read, and looked at Lucia. "What?"

"*Braid*, not brain," Lucia said. Then she did some more editing with her pinky.

They left the site feeling far less spooked than they originally had. Max led, since he knew how to cut through and find the path that went straight to the folly. Lucia carried Chester the whole way because he was dragging his poor fifth leg along the underbrush, but also because she was so grateful to him for being a cat without a cat carrier.

"When we get you back to Little Tunks," she whispered to Chester, "you'll have a garden full of other cats to fight with and mice to torture and when you're tired of it all, you can come inside and we'll spoil you silly." She whispered this so as not to remind Otto of Little Tunks in case he changed his mind.

Once in the folly, they heard tinny music playing from somewhere inside. They followed the sound up a set of stairs and down a hall until they spotted a swirl of colour through the doors of a little round tower room. The carousel was turning, the beautiful polished horses sliding up and down on their poles in front of the smiling royal family. Haddie was perched on a white horse with a red mane flying backwards in little twists, and she was talking on the phone. She sounded annoyed.

"If I make them go back to Little Tunks now, don't you think they'll start asking questions. They're not stupid kids, you know, and anyway maybe it's time they got some answers. They're old enough to handle it. And Otto already knows. What? Yes, I'm sure he knows, I'm positively sure . . ." The rest was lost because Haddie's horse had spun around to the other side of the carousel, away from the Hardscrabbles. When she came around next she noticed them standing there, smiled a tight little smile, and mouthed, "Your dad."

They each felt a sudden lump of disappointment in their bellies. It wasn't that they were unhappy to hear from their father. It was just that hearing from their father meant he had tracked them down and now he'd likely ship them back to Mrs. Carnival pronto.

"As a matter of fact, they've just come in, Casper," Haddie said into the phone. "You can talk to them your—" then Haddie disappeared momentarily as the horse spun around the other side. When she appeared again, she was holding out the phone. None of the Hardscrabbles stepped forward, so Haddie tossed the phone into the air. Six hands reached out to save it because somehow it was like she had thrown their father in the air. Lucia caught it. Then she realized the trick and tried to hand the phone off to her brothers, but they had backed up and waved their hands against the thing.

"Oh, fine," she said, glowering. She took a breath and put the phone to her ear.

"Hi, Dad."

"Lucia!" he said in the same way people say, "Thank heavens!"

It gave Lucia an idea.

"We were *stranded* in London, Dad!" She tried to sound traumatized. "Angela wasn't there—"

"Yes, yes, Haddie told me," he said,

"And there was this awful man covered with tattoos and he roughed up Otto."

"Good heavens, is he all right?"

"Yes, but we had to literally run for our lives."

"Oh, Lucia, I'm so sorry. I was rushing when I called Angela and it was all a stupid mistake—"

"We left our bags and everything under a tree, including our return tickets. We were too terrified to go back for them." She paused here, waiting for a sound of sympathy. It came as a sort of moan.

Haddie had slipped off her horse and turned off the carousel to hear better.

"But thank heavens, Haddie took us in," Lucia went on. "If she hadn't, well think. I mean, *think*!"

This may have been overly dramatic. Lucia noticed Haddie wince.

"Now look, Lucia." Casper's sympathetic tone took a sudden nosedive. "It's a lucky thing that you all are fine, and even that you wound up at Haddie's, although I still don't understand how *that* happened. But you need to return to Little Tunks right away. Tell Haddie to buy you all tickets back and I'll tell Mrs. Carnival to expect you this evening on the six o'clock train."

Lucia thought very swiftly and decided that, at this juncture, a straightforward approach would be the best.

"Why don't you like Haddie?" Lucia asked.

"It's not that I don't—is she standing right there? She's standing right there, isn't she, Lucia?"

"Yes," Lucia murmured, now convinced she had taken the exact wrong approach.

The phone was suddenly yanked out of her hands.

"Lucia's been out in the sun all morning," Haddie said into the phone. "I think she's a bit dehydrated. Now, listen, Casper, they're perfectly fine here. Why not let them stay? I promise I'll keep them out of trouble."

There was a long silence, during which Haddie said, "Yes," "I know," and "Understood," and then finally Haddie hung up.

"He says you can stay until tomorrow. Then he's coming to pick you up himself and take you back home."

"Tomorrow?" Max wailed.

"But it's not enough time!" Lucia said.

"No, it isn't. Not nearly," Haddie said, and she smiled

186

very sadly. It wasn't at all like the gentle and adoring smile of Empress Amalie of Schwartzenstadt-Russeldorf, but for some reason each Hardscrabble suddenly felt a soft pinch around their heart area, both achy and pleasant. Otto included.

Chapter 16

In which something awful happens
but I can't say what it is

The Hardscrabbles were so anxious to see if The Knee-bone Boy had eaten their food and seen their message—perhaps even left one of his own (although Max reminded them that it was unlikely, since he probably couldn't read or write)—that they had to keep from heading back to the woods immediately. They busied themselves, instead, by searching the folly. If they had to leave tomorrow, at least they might discover a secret passageway. They travelled the same confusing tangle of hallways and went up and down the illogical stairwells, just as they had when they searched for the passageway yesterday. Only today, they had Otto with them. Max and Lucia were positive that he would find it. Plus, they were armed with a hint from Mr. Pickering. He had heard the *tap-tap-tap*ping sound, then scraping, then the hiss before they'd entered the passageway.

"By the way, Otto," Max said as they walked down a hallway, "what is it that you already know?"

"What?" he asked.

"Haddie told Dad that you already knew something. What is it?"

"How should I know what she's talking about?" Otto answered. It instantly plunged him in a bad mood, so Lucia brought the subject back around to the task at hand.

"I'm guessing that the scraping sound was probably a panel that the Dusty Old Children slid open," she said. "And the tapping . . . don't you think we ought to have a go at tapping the walls, Otto?"

Otto didn't answer. He was standing perfectly still now while Chester weaved around his ankles lazily.

"What is it, Otto?" Lucia asked. She was half afraid that he was going to bolt out of the folly again and head for the train station.

"I think we should go this way," he said and he turned so suddenly that Chester sprang away. Swiftly, Otto made his way down the hallway and hurried down a staircase, followed by Lucia and Max. At the bottom of the stairs he turned left, walked some distance down the hallway, then turned around and walked back the other way. Finally they found themselves in the Great Hall. It was a bit of a disappointment. The Great Hall was their least favorite room, with its sneaky educational banners. Lucia couldn't imagine a less likely place to stick a secret passageway.

Yet this appeared to be the room that Otto was looking for. He walked across the flagstone floor, past the long table, and he stopped directly in front of the grandfather clock.

"What? Do you mean it's behind the clock?" Lucia said.

"There's something behind it, I don't know what," he said. "I had that feeling the last time we were here, but I pushed it out of my head."

"Well, the tap-tap-tapping might be the sound of a clock, I guess," Max said thoughtfully. "It's not working now, but it might have been when the Dusty Old Children were here. And the scraping . . . maybe they were pushing it and the passageway is behind it."

So they started to push against the grandfather clock. It was heavy and awkward. Twice it tipped scarily, but they steadied it in time. Bit by bit they managed to shove it to one side, enough to reveal a small door set in the wall. The door was just big enough for any of them to squeeze through, no bigger. It had a curious brass latch with a yellowy white button on it that looked like it was made of bone.

After a moment's hesitation, all three of them lunged forward to press the button. Lucia's finger hit it first. The door flew open and a silver head burst out, carried on a long neck with spiked flares on either side. The creature's glistening black lips were curled back to expose two rows of serrated teeth. Its eyes were cat yellow with rippled pupils under a lumpy brow pitched low with fury.

The Hardscrabbles dashed to the table and ducked behind the chairs right before the mouth snapped wide-open and spat out a long, furious flame. To their horror,

Chester had stayed where he was by the hidden door, his back arched and hair on end as he hissed at the thing.

Otto lurched forward to rescue Chester but Lucia caught his shirt and held him back with all her strength. The dragon's neck flailed about madly, the flame whipping through the air, as though it were desperately seeking out hair to singe and flesh to burn. Chester flattened himself against the ground—clever cat—and the flame whooshed over him. The dragon thrashed on and on, its fury seeming to increase as its attempts to burn were frustrated, until its head suddenly withdrew back into the depths of the little doorway. The door slammed shut.

Immediately, Otto ran for Chester. Lucia let him. She could barely stand up herself, she was that shaky. Max's face was damp with sweat and quite pink, but his eyes had that stupid look that they got when he was thinking deeply and importantly.

A small keening sound came from Otto as he clutched Chester, his hand stroking the top of the black head over and over. Lucia had heard him make a sound like that once or twice before but he had always been asleep when he did.

"Oh, poor thing!" Lucia cried out and she rushed over to Otto and wrapped her arms around him. He stopped making the noise instantly—I don't think he realized he was making it at all till then—and Lucia carefully added, "Poor cat!" So he let Lucia hug him, both of them pretending that it was Chester whom she was fussing over.

Once they had all settled down and had left the Great

Hall and reconvened outside in the comforting sunshine of the courtyard, Lucia grew angry.

"They're mad! The stupid Kneebones. Mad and cruel! Who puts something like that in a kids' castle?"

"It wasn't real, you know," Max said. "It was just a mechanical toy, like the dungeon rat."

"Well, obviously, it wasn't an *actual* dragon." Lucia's nostrils puffed out. "But the fire was quite actual, thank you very much. We might have been roasted! And then there's poor Chester who very nearly was."

Poor Chester had recovered from the incident nicely and was now stalking something in the grass.

"And," Lucia continued, "we're still no closer to finding the secret passageway."

"Maybe we should check at the birch trees again," Otto suggested. "To see if The Kneebone Boy has eaten the food."

Dragons and monsters. You see how easily they are talking about such things, when not a few days before the Hardscrabbles' lives were rather boring and rubbishy? It's alarming how quickly people adjust to adventures when they are in one. You have to really work at being astonished by life.

The Hardscrabbles set off for the woods once again, this time Max leading the way because he said he remembered how to get back to the right spot. He did. They arrived at the birch trees quickly and without any backtracking.

Someone had been there. The napkin had been unrolled and lay across the empty plate, and the soda and bag of crisps were gone. The Hardscrabbles looked all around them, even up at the trees, before they stepped closer. Their message on the rock had been wiped out and now there was a new message written with a wet finger in the Pixy Stix powder: GOOD CRISPS.

The writing was a little wobbly, which of course may have been because The Kneebone Boy had never written in Pixy Stix powder, but it might also have been because of misshapen hands, alias claws.

The Hardscrabbles looked at the rock then at one another with wide eyes. Lucia giggled. You'll understand why if you think about it.

"Well, now we know he can read and write," Max said, sounding relieved.

"That's good." Lucia felt the same way. If he could read and write, he was somehow more human, less monster.

"At least someone cared enough to teach him," Otto said, which was of course the right and compassionate way to see it, and Lucia and Max nodded thoughtfully.

Otto glanced at Chester. His tail hung down in a very relaxed way.

"He's not anywhere nearby," Otto said.

Then they set out four more sandwiches and Lucia even picked a spray of flowers and laid it on the other side of the plate and they sat there and waited.

"I was thinking," Max said, "about how this will all end."

"What do you mean?" Lucia asked. She didn't like the sound of that.

"Well, it's all very well to feed him," Max explained. "And maybe we can even make friends with him. But then what? We'll have to go home tomorrow and what will happen to him when we do?"

"He'll come with us," Otto replied automatically.

"That's ridiculous!" Max said.

"Why?" Otto said.

"For a hundred different reasons," Max cried.

"Well, he can't keep living the way he does, locked away in a room," Otto protested.

"And what are we supposed to do with him in Little Tunks?" Max replied. "Everyone already thinks that *you're* a monster! What happens when we bring *him* home with us?"

It was a dreadful thing to say, especially because it was true. Max regretted it instantly but it was too late, and anyway he was bound to say it sooner or later. Lucia was so outraged that she couldn't speak, but Otto's hands began to move very calmly and beautifully.

"*I* don't mind people like The Kneebone Boy," he said. "I don't mind monsters."

Max was silent for a good long while. He scratched at the nape of his neck, he tapped his fist on his thigh. He wasn't thinking deeply and importantly; he kept very still when he did that. Instead he was imagining "how it would all end." There are so many possible endings for an adventure. They are all interesting except for one: the one in which in the end, everything is pretty much exactly the way it was at the very beginning.

"It's going to be dead cramped in our bedroom with three people," Max said finally.

So everything was all right. That is until they discovered that it wasn't.

"Where's Chester?" Lucia asked.

Chapter 17

I'm not telling you a single thing about
this chapter because it will ruin everything

They searched everywhere for Chester, calling out his name. It was baffling. One minute he was there, and the next he wasn't.

"He probably saw a squirrel and went off after it, then got lost," Max said lightly. He was perfectly fond of Chester, but he wasn't really an animal person.

Otto shook his head, troubled. "He wouldn't have gone that far."

"How do you know?" Max said. "He might be one of those cats that disappears for days then comes back smelling of dead things."

"What bothers me is the traps," Lucia said suddenly.

Her brothers looked at her.

"Saint George's traps," she explained. "Maybe Chester got caught in one of them."

"What kind of traps were they?" Otto asked.

Lucia shrugged. "He didn't say."

"He must have dug holes," Max said after thinking a minute. "Deep ones that are covered with brush and leaves, so he could catch The Kneebone Boy without maiming him."

"Chester might have fallen in one of those," Lucia said.

Now they kept their eyes on the ground as they walked, watching for holes and calling Chester's name, then listening for an answering meow.

There was something that they were all thinking, but none of them wanted to say it. It was too horrible. Still, I'll tell you what it was because I've told you everything else so far: They all wondered if it was The Kneebone Boy who had snatched Chester and had perhaps done something gruesome to him. They hated to think this thought because they all were cheering so hard for The Kneebone Boy, you understand, and they had already decided that they would help him at all costs, so it seemed very disloyal to consider that he might have gutted Chester. Still, they did consider it and it made them all feel very anxious.

After a solid twenty minutes of wandering, Max stopped and said, "This is silly. We should split up to cover more ground."

Lucia said that Otto should stay with her, since he couldn't call out if he got lost. But Max said that Otto should stay with him, because Max was no good with animals and if he should come upon Chester stuck in a tight spot, he wouldn't be able to coax him out. It made the most sense, of course, even if Lucia didn't like it.

We'll stick with her now as she wades through the thick brush, all alone.

Lucia kept her eyes on the ground, watching for suspicious-looking clumps of twigs or leaves that might be covering a pit. She found a few clumps but when she pushed at them with the toe of her shoe, they really were only clumps. As she walked she called out and listened, until she gradually began thinking about that thing that none of them had wanted to think about. It's one thing to not think certain thoughts when you are with other people; it's a whole other thing to not think them when you are by yourself and the wind is picking up.

Lucia felt that defenseless sensation at the back of her neck again. She began to pay more attention to the shadows all around her rather than the clumps of leaves and twigs on the ground. Above her head, the branches began to slap each other fitfully and the leaves made *ahhh* noises, as though thousands of tiny people were hanging from them and sighing all at once. It was eerie and magical at the same time. Lucia stopped to listen, gazing around at the swaying green and silver underbrush.

If I were The Kneebone Boy, Lucia thought, this is where I'd want to stay. Right here, deep in the woods where there are no eyes to gawk at me. I could slip along the ground like a shadow, hidden because the woods loves to hide things, not because it's ashamed of them. I wouldn't want to go to Little Tunks, either, even if people were kind to me and I had a nice, soft bed. I'd just want to live here forever, with the foxes and hedgehogs and the wild mush-rooms under my toes.

It was then that Lucia heard the voice from high in the treetop. It said, "Don't look up."

You can't imagine how hard it is not to look up when a voice from the treetops tells you not to. Lucia lifted her head, just the smallest bit, and the voice said, "If you look up, I'll go away."

"I won't, I promise," Lucia said and she pointed her face directly at the ground. She was scared, but not as scared as you might expect her to be. It was all so unreal, you understand. It was almost like reading a story about yourself.

"Are you—" She almost said The Kneebone Boy, but stopped herself in time. That wasn't his real name, after all. He did have a real name—Mr. Pickering had said it—but for the life of her she couldn't remember what it was. Instead she said, "You live in the castle, don't you?" she said.

"I don't *live* there. I'm *kept* there," he said.

"I'm sorry," Lucia replied and she started to look up without thinking. There was a great shuffling in the treetop and leaves fluttered down as The Kneebone Boy started to scramble away.

"No, no, please don't go!" Lucia cried. The sounds settled and the woods grew quiet again.

Then The Kneebone Boy said, "The younger boy . . . he's clever, isn't he?"

"Max, you mean? Yes," Lucia admitted. "Sometimes very."

The Kneebone Boy's voice was unexpected. Somehow, Lucia imagined it would be deep and garbled as though it were struggling out of a twisted body. Instead, his voice was soft and clear.

"I thought so," The Kneebone Boy said. "And the tall, blond boy . . . something is wrong with him."

Lucia bristled at this. "There's nothing wrong with Otto," she snapped.

"Good, good." The Kneebone Boy's voice soothed. "It's good you stick up for him."

Lucia remembered that The Kneebone Boy had nobody to stick up for *him*, and she immediately felt sorry that she had lost her temper.

There was a sudden scratching sound, like a squirrel scrambling down a tree and it took all of Lucia's self-control to keep her eyes on the ground. In a moment, out of the corner of her eye, she saw a black shadow creeping toward her. Then she felt something rub against her ankles with a mewling sound.

"Chester!" she cried. She squatted down to pick him up and she buried her face in his fur. "Oh, sweet, sweet Chester," Lucia said into his fur, smiling as she pictured Otto's face when she returned with Chester in her arms.

"He was following me," The Kneebone Boy said. "I didn't take him." Just as though he knew what she'd been thinking, which made her very ashamed.

"Listen," Lucia said, "we've been talking, my brothers and I, and we decided that you should come home with us. Our house isn't anything special, but we do have a garden and our dad's quite nice."

She had not forgotten her thoughts about how The Kneebone Boy should stay in the woods; but she had thought them before she had met him, and now that he was here and real and speaking to her, she couldn't bear to think of leaving him to roam the woods only to be caught and locked up again, or to be made into a spectacle by Saint George.

The Kneebone Boy didn't say anything for so long that Lucia asked, "Are you still there?"

There was a hiss of shifting leaves. "Yes," he said. "I was just thinking."

"About what?" Lucia asked.

"The garden. Do you think it's big enough for a peacock to live in?"

"I don't know," Lucia said, surprised by the question. "I suppose so. Peacocks aren't very huge, are they? So will you? Will you come back with us?"

"I think . . . yes, I'd like to," The Kneebone Boy said.

"Good. Excellent!" Lucia fisted up her hands and they gave a little bob of happiness. "Our father will be here tomorrow. Meet us in the morning by the two birch trees, where we left the food. All right?"

"All right," The Kneebone Boy said.

"Until then, mind about the traps—"

What made Lucia look off to the right at that moment, she'll never know. Certainly there was no sound. Creeping stealthily through the woods, his rifle in hand, was Saint George.

"Go, go, go! He's coming!" Lucia cried in a low voice, and in her alarm she forgot her promise and looked up at The Kneebone Boy.

He was lying across the upper branch of a tree like a leopard, dressed in a soiled white robe. When their eyes met he did not move a muscle but his eyes went wide. So did Lucia's. His face was dirty, his hair wild-looking. Still, Lucia recognized him immediately.

From his high perch, the Sultan of Juwi brought a finger to his lips and in a moment he was gone.

Chapter 18

In which we find out something about
Otto's scarf and take a peek inside
the Hardscrabbles' brains

"What are you doing here?" Saint George demanded, glancing all around him suspiciously.

Still stunned by what she had just seen, Lucia looked at him without answering.

"Who were you talking to?" Saint George asked.

"Nobody," Lucia said, finding her voice.

"I heard you. You were talking to someone."

"To the cat," Lucia said feebly.

There was the sound of quick footsteps approaching and Otto and Max appeared, looking pink in the face. Upon seeing Chester, Otto smiled broadly and grabbed him out of Lucia's arms, then tucked him beneath his scarf.

"We thought we heard voices," Max said. "Oh, hello," he said to Saint George.

"Now you lot had better listen to me," Saint George

said, a thick finger pointing around at all of them. "You keep out of these woods. It's property of the castle. If you need to get to the town, keep to the path, but quit stomping through here."

"Oh, excuse me, *Lord Kneebone*," Lucia said smartly. "I thought you were just a shopkeeper who, by the way, is *also* trespassing."

He glowered at her in a way that made her want to take a step backward. She didn't though. After making a low sound of disgust in his throat, he shoved past them and started off again, muttering, "If I were their aunt, I'd throw them all in the dungeon and toss the key into the abyss."

When Saint George was safely out of earshot, Lucia turned to her brothers.

"He was here," she said. "Up in that tree." Her voice sounded odd even to herself. It was light and faraway, like she was recounting a dream.

"*He?*" Max said. "Do you mean The Kneebone Boy?"

Lucia hesitated. It felt like a very, very long hesitation to her, but it was no more than a couple of seconds.

"Yes."

"Did you talk to him? What happened? Did he have Chester?" Otto asked.

"Yes, Chester was with him," Lucia said. "We talked a little. He'll meet us by the birch trees tomorrow."

"You sound funny," Otto said.

"Did you actually see him then?" Max asked, wincing in expectation of a description.

"No," Lucia said. "I never did."

You are wondering why Lucia is not telling her brother that The Kneebone Boy is, in fact, the Sultan of Juwi. She has a good reason and it is this: They would not have believed her. Maybe you don't believe her either. After all, she does have a tendency to see bits and pieces of the sultan in other people. There is no denying that Mr. Dupuis has the sultan's chin and eyes. And her classmate Aidan McMartin has the Sultan's lower lip, but exactly. Then there was the woman on the train. . . . They all have bits and pieces of the sultan but the boy in the tree *was* the sultan, every bit and piece of him, right down to the quick-primed eyes that looked as though they knew all Lucia's worst qualities and liked her even more because of them.

If she had told her brothers about the sultan and they didn't believe that she had seen him, she ran the risk of not believing that she had seen him either. And she *must* believe she has seen him. Too much depends upon it in order for this story to come out right.

"Here's to our last night together!" Haddie tapped her Coke can against each of theirs. "You have been exemplary prisoners. You shall be sorely missed."

"But won't we see you again?" Max said, without drinking to the toast.

"That's up to your father,"—Haddie threw back her head and swigged down some soda—"and if he finds you healthy and happy and all in one piece tomorrow." She quickly scrutinized them all. "None of you have major abrasions or missing fingers, I assume?"

They shook their heads.

"Hmm." Haddie seemed slightly disappointed. "Then maybe we should raise the stakes a little."

After supper Haddie fetched a box of fireworks that she had found stuffed up one of the fireplaces, probably by one of the Dusty Old Children as a prank for some poor servant who went to light a fire. ("What stinkers!" Haddie said. "I like those Kneebone kids more and more, even if they were pigs.")

They carried the box up the stairs and outside, to one of the walkways on top of the curtain wall. It was an excellent night for fireworks—clear and black and shot through with stars. From the walkway there was a fine view of Kneebone Castle, its lumpy, misshapen silhouette pitted with light from several windows.

Haddie lit the first firecracker. It was a dud. All it did was make a *thwipp* sound then fizzle out.

"Do you miss your mother very much?" Haddie asked them suddenly as she pulled out another firecracker from the box and handed it to Otto.

The question rankled Lucia. It felt sneaky. It made her want to say, "If you *are* her, why don't you just say so already! Say so, and we can be furious at you and make you cry and then we can forgive you!"

Instead, she answered with perfect composure, "We manage."

But Max could not contain himself, of course. "We miss her every day," he said, looking at Haddie ardently.

"And you?" Haddie turned to Otto.

Otto would not meet her eyes. He just stared down at the firecracker as he toyed with it.

"All right," said Haddie, "then tell me this." She suddenly reached out and grabbing the end of his scarf, she gave it a sharp tug. "What's the deal with the scarf?"

Otto raised his right hand. Max and Lucia flinched. But instead of attacking Haddie, Otto rubbed his right hand across his chest, held his left pinky up and bent it down twice, then touched it to his chin.

"What did he say?" Haddie looked to Lucia for a translation.

Lucia frowned, perplexed. "He says that Mum gave him her scarf before she left."

Otto's hands started moving again while Lucia and Max watched them carefully.

"He says, the night before she disappeared Mum came into his room. She knelt beside his bed and tied the scarf around his neck. It was her special scarf. Then she told him to wear it always, and no matter what happened to her, no matter where she had to go, she would one day see the scarf and they would know each other by it."

Haddie smiled at Otto.

"Good boy," she said. Her eyes looked suspiciously moist. So you see, they did make her cry after all, just a little bit.

They set off the rest of the firecrackers, and a couple of them went off beautifully, lighting up the black sky and even illuminating Kneebone Castle across the way. The drawbridge was down tonight and more lights flicked on throughout the castle, perhaps because of the strange spectacle of fireworks, yet it looked as grim as always.

"Have you ever met the Kneebones?" Lucia asked Haddie, who was staring at the castle too.

"Of course not," Haddie said. "The Kneebones don't live there anymore. They haven't in years."

All the Hardscrabbles turned to her in surprise.

"But you said they were living there now," Lucia objected.

"I never did," Haddie replied.

"She's right," Max said after thinking for a bit. "She never did. We just assumed."

"Local gossip is, the Kneebones lost all their money almost ten years ago. They sold everything, castle and folly included," Haddie said.

"Then who owns the castle now?" Lucia asked,

"A doctor. What's his name . . . what's his name? . . . Oh! Azziz," Haddie said. "Dr. Azziz."

"Dr. Azziz!" Lucia and Max cried out at the same time. They looked at each other in confusion.

"Do you know him?" Haddie asked as she reached for the last firecracker in the box.

"No," Lucia said quickly. It wasn't exactly a lie.

The last firecracker was a disappointment. It made a loud crack but after a brief flash of light it sputtered right out. Kneebone Castle was absorbed back into the night. They stood there for a few minutes, staring out into blackness, thin wisps of smoke from the fireworks still lolling about the sky. In the distance they could hear the sound of dogs barking—an ordinary nighttime sound, but in the gloom it seemed ominous. Even Haddie's mood turned somber as she tipped her head up and listened. When she caught them watching her, she shooed them off the battlement.

"All right, fun's over. Off to bed," she said. They weren't sorry to go. They were fairly bursting to talk to one another in the privacy of the dungeon about what they had learned. Lucia turned back once, only to see Haddie pacing the battlement, her hands shoved in the pockets of her jeans and her eyes fixed on the ground below. Much like a sentry who suspects that a siege is imminent.

"Do you think it could be the same Dr. Azziz who murdered the sultan's family?" Otto asked once they were in the dungeon.

"I think it is *exactly* the same Dr. Azziz," Lucia replied fiercely. She was walking around the perimeter of the dungeon wall, while her brothers were sitting on Otto's bed. She couldn't remain still; her thoughts were tumbling over themselves. Every so often the rat popped out of the wall and skittered across the floor, but Lucia stepped over it and kept walking.

"It might just be a coincidence," Max said. "And another thing . . . we must have been wrong about The Kneebone Boy. He wouldn't still be here if all the Kneebones left years ago."

"We *were* totally wrong about The Kneebone Boy," Lucia said, stopping and facing her brothers.

Now she could tell her story. Timing is everything, as they say.

Instead of making fun of her for having seen the sultan, Otto and Max listened carefully. After she had finished they said nothing for a good three minutes as they tried to imagine what it all meant.

"Then you think Dr. Azziz has been keeping the sultan in the tower?" Max asked Lucia.

"I'm one hundred percent sure of it," Lucia replied.

Actually, she was only about 87 percent sure of it, but try saying you are 87 percent sure of something with conviction. You can't.

Max nodded. "That's quite a common strategy, the most famous of course being Richard the Third, who imprisoned the two young heirs to the throne in the Tower of London and then had them murdered."

"Imagine what might have happened if we hadn't—"

"Think what Dad will say when he sees him—"

They each climbed into bed and said good night to one another, and pretended to be falling sleep. Instead, they were all busy thinking.

Here is some of what Otto thought:

> *I wonder what happened to The Kneebone Boy.*
>
> *The sultan can take my bed and I'll bring up the spare mattress from the basement.*
>
> *I once read about an albino peacock.*

My neck itches.
I hear those dogs barking again.

Now Max:

I wonder if the sultan likes rooftops. I know he likes treetops. He'll probably like rooftops.

I wonder if Haddie likes rooftops. Will Haddie come home with us as well? She will. She has to.

She doesn't smell of mountain mint gum. She smells of peanut butter.

I shouldn't have called Otto a monster. Now I feel especially rotten after what he said about Mum and the scarf. Not that I ever believed the story about him strangling her with it. Not really.

Funny thing about the Abyss . . . (he is thinking deeply and importantly about something now, but I won't tell you what it is because it will spoil things later.)

Why are those dogs barking like that?

And finally Lucia:

If the sultan sees the sketch of himself on my bedroom wall, will he think I fancy him? I mean I do, but not like I fancy Mr. Dupuis.

I can't believe I said that.

No, I don't.

Yes, I do.

It's different with the sultan though.

Otto is scratching at something. He probably got a rash from the woods.

How strange about the scarf! Why didn't Mum leave a scarf for me as well?

When Dad comes here, I'll investigate his face at the very moment he sets eyes on Haddie. That will show whether or not she is Mum. If she is, he'll smile from the right side of his mouth. His left side is for when he thinks you're being ridiculous.

Oh, for heaven's sake, when will those dogs shut up?

The barking had become increasingly frantic, rising and falling in pitch but never ceasing. Chester leapt off Otto's bed and sat below the window far above, his silky black ears tuning this way and that.

"Cor, it sounds like there's a dozen of them!" Max said out loud.

"It sounds like they've caught something," Lucia said. Then a second later she sat up in bed and cried out, "No!"

Jumping out of bed, she began to pull on her trainers. "The sultan! They must have sent dogs after him! Come on, come on, we can't let them catch him!"

Otto and Max leapt out of bed and in no time the Hard-scrabbles had jammed on their trainers, not bothering with socks, and straightaway rushed out of the dungeon, still dressed in their Snoring-by-the-Sea pyjamas. Well, not perfectly straightaway. There was a hasty discussion about bringing Chester, but they decided it was too risky because of the dogs, so they shut him in the dungeon, though they hated to do it. They ran up the stairs and wound their way around the hallways, backtracking once to grab a torch that hung on a hook, and finally emerged outside in the courtyard. A brisk wind fluttered their pyjama tops and crept up underneath, chilling them to their armpits. Outside, the noise of the dogs baying sounded closer than before. They could hear voices as well—too distant to make out the words, but the voices sounded urgent and excited. It made the Hardscrabbles' hearts quicken and they ran even faster, across the grassy courtyard and over the drawbridge, which thankfully was already lowered.

The moment they entered the woods, instinct made them slow down. The night was so black it was almost shadowless. They picked their way along carefully, shining the torch on the ground and heading in the direction of the twin birches. They hadn't gone far when the barking tapered off, then stopped altogether. In its place came a cry that brought them to a standstill—a human cry so full of anguish that all the Hardscrabbles clamped their hands over their mouths, as though they were trying to stop that horrible sound from entering their own bodies.

"They caught him," Otto said. Although his hands were barely visible in the darkness, Lucia and Max understood.

Soon there was the sound of approaching voices and the loud, brash footsteps of people who didn't care if they were heard. The Hardscrabbles ducked behind a thicket and crouched low. They watched in silence, holding their breaths when they saw the black outline of dogs attached to leads. To be honest, there weren't a dozen dogs, as they'd imagined. There were only two. But they were really large. Then came the men holding the leads, and two others. In the midst of them, surrounded on all sides, was the small, slender figure of the sultan.

One of the dogs lifted his nose in the Hardscrabbles' direction and let out a sharp bark, but the man who held his lead yanked it hard to quiet him.

If you're expecting the Hardscrabbles to do something brave at this point, you'll be disappointed. Remember that this is a true story with true kids who would no more have ambushed those men than you would. Anyway, it would have been a silly thing to do. They would have been instantly clobbered and we would never get to the most exciting bits that are coming quite soon.

(Mr. Dupuis says it is a cheap trick for an author to promise that exciting things are about to happen. He says it is the mark of an insecure writer who is afraid that readers might put the book down. He's wrong in this case though. I just wanted to give you a heads-up. I'm dead positive that you won't put this book down now, since you've read through some boring parts during which you might have, and anyway you're not stupid enough to stop reading right when we are about to sneak into Kneebone Castle.)

(Mr. Dupuis says I shouldn't bully readers by calling them stupid.)

(I'm not saying you *are* stupid though. Just if you put the book down.)

"I've been thinking," Max said when the men disappeared once again into the darkness.

Lucia and Otto turned to him eagerly. They had not been thinking. They had only been feeling awful.

"I've been thinking about the dragon in the Great Hall," Max said.

"Well, that's useless," Lucia said.

"And how, in stories, dragons are always guarding something important," Max continued, ignoring her. "Like piles of gold or a kidnapped princess. I'll bet that door behind the grandfather clock is the secret passageway—the one that the Dusty Old Children used in order to visit The Kneebone Boy—and that's why the dragon is guarding it."

Lucia and Otto considered this.

"Still perfectly useless," Lucia decided, "unless you want to barbeque yourself."

"But the Dusty Old Children got in," Otto said to her.

"Exactly," said Max. "And I think I know how they did it."

They waited for to him to tell them.

"Are you going to tell us?" Lucia said after a few moments.

"It's just an educated guess. I'll tell you when I'm sure."

"That's not fair," Lucia said.

"You did the same thing when you thought you saw the sultan," Max said. He stood up and wiped soil off his shins. "Right. I'm going to town."

"What? Now?" Lucia said.

"Has to be now. We're leaving tomorrow so we have to rescue the sultan tonight." He started walking. "You two go back to the folly. I'll be there later."

"You're going to walk through the woods in the middle of the night by yourself?" Lucia said.

"I don't mind," Max said.

So Lucia and Otto were forced to not mind either. That was how they found themselves picking their way through the woods, going who knows where, to do who knows what, dressed in pyjamas with lavender hippos on their bums.

If there are illustrations in this book, I'd prefer that this last part not be shown.

Chapter 19

*In which Max's educated guess had better
be right or else Lucia and Otto
are going to throttle him*

The whole way to town, the Hardscrabbles' arms and legs were tortured by thistles and scratched by bushes and poked in rude places by branches. There were many outbursts of "Ouch bloody ouch!" and "That nearly took out my eye!" and once, "A snake went down my shirt . . . a snake went down my shirt . . . *a snake went down my shirt!!*"

I won't tell you who screamed that last thing.

But you'd think someone who was supposedly so intelligent could tell the difference between a snake and an acorn.

By the time they arrived in town, they had leaves in their hair and scratches all over their legs, some of which were bleeding. They walked down the streets hoping no one would be out, but wouldn't you know it, a car suddenly pulled up to the curb just ahead of them, its radio pounding out music. The engine and the music stopped. The doors were flung open and six loud teenagers piled out.

"Oh crap," Lucia whispered. The last people you want to run into when you are walking around in public dressed in matching pyjamas are teenagers. The Hardscrabbles looked around for a hiding place and saw a chunky hedge that might do, but before they could duck behind it, the teenagers spotted them.

"Hello, what's this?" one of them said. "The plonker triplets?"

They all found this hysterically funny, slapping one another on the backs and saying, "Good one, yeah?" They hooted and laughed and staggered around like a pack of drunken idiots as the Hardscrabbles walked by.

If I ever become like this when I am a teenager, I hope someone smothers me in my sleep.

Eventually, the Hardscrabbles came to Saint George's Taxidermy & Curiosities shop. Much to Lucia's horror, Max went right up to the door and knocked on it.

"You can't be serious?" she cried.

He ignored her as he stood on tiptoes and tried to peer through the window on the door. "I think I see him way in the back." He knocked again more loudly.

"What's he doing? Torturing hamsters?" Lucia asked.

Max suddenly took a few steps back from the door, clasped his hands behind his back, and waited at attention.

A lock clicked and the door opened. Lucia had the distinct impression that Saint George may have heard that last part. He appeared at the doorway, black apron on, and half a dozen marbles cupped in one hand. His face was pinched with annoyance as he looked them over, taking in their state of dress and the snaky dried trickles of blood on their legs.

"What happened to you?" he said.

"We need help," Max said.

"Yeah, you do," he replied and started to close the door.

"We need to get past the dragon in the Great Hall," Max said quickly, before the door shut in his face.

Saint George paused. If he hadn't had a face like a Viking, you would have thought he was blushing.

"Piss off," he said. He shut the door and locked it.

"Oh, yes, well done, Max," Lucia said. But Max didn't look at all defeated. On the contrary, he looked extremely self-satisfied.

"I was right," Max said quietly, but before Otto or Lucia could ask, "About what?" Max had started to hurry around to the back of the shop in a very determined way.

Lucia and Otto followed, mostly out of pure curiosity. Now they could see the barn where Saint George's ponies must be kept, a tumble-down affair surrounded by a small fenced pasture. Max opened a latched gate and walked through the tiny pasture to a window in the back of the shop. If they jumped, they could grab fleeting glimpses of what was evidently the workshop, a dingy little room whose walls were covered with animal skins. There were rows and rows of shelves filled with glues and paints and whatnot, and in the middle of it all was Saint George, perched on a stool with his back to them. In front of him was the head of a deer stuck on a metal stand. Saint George dug around in a plastic cup that was wedged between his legs and he pulled out an amber-coloured marble. He held it up to the light and studied it for a moment before placing it in the deer's empty eye socket.

Lucia let out a sound of disgust, which made Saint George look up from his work. The Hardscrabbles had been jumping up and down in order to see into the window, so when Saint George turned around he saw Otto's head for a second before it disappeared, then Lucia's head, then Max's head, then Max's head again, with a smile on its face. He said something they couldn't hear but I'm sure it was nothing that could be printed in a book that kids will read, so it's just as well. He got up out of his chair and the next glimpse they had was of an empty room.

"I told you to go home," Saint George said gruffly. He was suddenly standing right behind them, looking like he was cursing his Viking ancestors for not having done a more thorough job of wiping every last English person off the map.

"We will," Max said. "After you tell us what happened to The Kneebone Boy."

"He's skulking around in the woods, isn't he," Saint George said.

"That's not The Kneebone Boy and you know it."

"Max!" Lucia warned.

"What happened to the *real* Kneebone Boy?" Max asked.

Saint George didn't answer but he did look around, as though checking to see if anyone were listening.

"Did you ever let him out of the tower to play in the woods?" Max asked. "Mr. Pickering said you wanted to, but your brother and sister wouldn't do it."

"Pickering told you that!?"

"He didn't say your name," Max told him quickly. "But the thing is, I think a lot. I think about everything, especially if something doesn't make sense. I can't help it, ask *them*. And a lot of things about you didn't make sense, so I kept thinking until I figured it out."

"He's one of the Dusty Old Children?" Otto asked.

"The youngest one," Max said.

"Are you really a Kneebone?" Lucia asked Saint George. This was a rather fascinating turn of events.

"There's nothing amazing about it," Saint George said. "Most people in Snoring know who I am. I don't hide it."

"Yes, but do they know why you're called Saint George?" Max asked.

"Oh, why is he?" Lucia asked excitedly.

"Mr. Pickering said that before they went into the secret passageway, he heard a *tap-tap-tap*ping," said Max. "Well, that probably was the clock, just as we guessed. And the scraping must have been when they moved aside the clock to get to the cabinet. But the hiss above their heads . . . that was curious." Max was enjoying himself very obnoxiously now, but Lucia was too interested to be annoyed. "I kept thinking about that hiss and I thought of all the things that could fly over your head and make a hiss. Then I remembered the archery bows on the wall of the Great Hall. An arrow would make a hiss like that as it was shot over your head, wouldn't it? Someone might have shot the dragon with an arrow in order to get past it. And that made me think of the most famous dragon slayer of all, Saint George, isn't it, and the story about the dragon that made its nest at the spring of a city's water supply. The dragon wouldn't budge, so in order for the citizens to get their water they brought the King's daughter as a sacrifice. But just as the dragon is about to eat the princess, Saint George comes along and kills the dragon. I thought about that story. And then I started to think about Saint George, *this* Saint George, I mean, and all the things about him that didn't make sense."

It was all so much like the climax of a mystery novel, which as you know Lucia generally doesn't like, but when it's happening in real life it's quite impressive.

"For instance, Saint George's little white ponies. I guessed there wouldn't be a lot of room behind his shop to keep horses, even little ones and look, I was right. And little ponies like that . . . well it's usually old ladies in hats who keep them or else kids, not big, hulking men. But then Mr. Pickering mentioned the little ponies that the Dusty Old Children rode and I remembered that the funeral carriage was a miniature, like a play carriage for children.

"But it was something that *you* said"—he nodded toward Saint George, who was listening to it all with a harassed look on his face—"that made me quite sure about it all. Remember when you said that Haddie ought to lock us in the dungeon and toss the key into the Abyss. Well, I wondered how you would know about the Abyss in the first place. Mr. Pickering said no one ever went into the folly, and even if you had managed to poke around there, what are the chances that you would have found a little hole hidden behind a tapestry?

"So after much, much thinking I decided that you must be one of the Dusty Old Chi—I mean one of the Kneebones, and that you were the one to shoot the arrow into the dragon and disable him, which made your brother and sister nickname you Saint George."

"Is he right?" Lucia asked Saint George eagerly.

"No," Saint George said.

Even though Lucia generally enjoyed when Max was wrong about something, this was massively disappointing.

"My brother and sister didn't give me the nickname, I gave it to myself," Saint George said. He no longer looked angry, which is as close as possible to saying that he looked pleased. "I deserved the name too. I shot that dragon in the eye every time, and I'd even call left or right one before I nailed it."

The Hardscrabbles smiled at one another.

"You'll help us to get past the dragon then?" Max said.

"No," Saint George said. They waited for him to say that he was just joking, but he didn't.

"But why not?" Lucia finally asked.

"Because the secret passageway is dangerous. Because there's no bloody reason for me to do it. And because even if I wanted to, I can't," Saint George replied.

"You mean you've lost your knack?" Lucia asked.

"No, I've lost my arrow," Saint George said. "It takes a

particular arrow, and that arrow was lost years ago. A regular one won't do."

"Does that arrow have a funny, jaggedy tip?" Max asked.

Saint George's eyes narrowed. "You've seen it?"

Max smiled. He'd be a terrible poker player. You're supposed to keep a straight face when you know you are holding the winning cards.

"Where?" Saint George asked.

"In the Abyss. Stuck in the dirt wall."

"You mean that old thing we found?" Lucia turned to Max in surprise.

"Idiots!" Saint George cried.

"Excuse me?" Lucia said, her nostrils expanding on the instant.

"Not you, not you," Saint George said hastily. "Do you have it with you?" he asked Max.

"It's back at the folly," Max said. "It's yours if you help us."

"It's mine in any case," he said.

"True," Max said, "but we know where it is, and you don't."

For a moment it seemed entirely possible that Saint George would pick Max up by the back of his shirt, and heave-ho him straight over the gate.

Instead, he asked, "Why do you want to go in the secret passageway in any case?"

This was a bit tricky, so of course Lucia and Otto looked at Max. Since he had worked out everything it seemed natural that he would have worked out this part as well. But to their shock and dismay, Max was looking right back at them imploringly.

Lucia pressed her lips together and composed herself with a sniff. Then she turned to Saint George and said, "Because it's a *secret passageway*, for goodness' sakes."

Saint George seemed to accept this explanation. After all, he had been one of the Dusty Old Children once, years ago.

"It's not a romp in a theme park," Saint George warned. "There are some treacherous bits."

"What would be the point of going in if there weren't?" Lucia said.

A small, smirky smile crept across Saint George's mouth.

"All right, I'll do it," he said. "I'll stop by in the morning. Now get out."

"No," Max said. "It has to be now. We're leaving tomorrow."

Saint George rolled his eyes. "All right then," he muttered, "Let's get this over with."

They followed him out the gate, but he stopped suddenly and turned around. He looked them up and down, taking in their state of dress and their various scraped-up arms and legs. Then he sighed.

"I suppose you'll want to take a carriage rather than walk?" he said.

"Yes, please," they answered promptly.

Chapter 20

In which the Hardscrabbles admit
they are not normal, not at all

T hough the stable looked rough from the outside, inside
it was clean and smelled of that yeasty hay-and-horse
smell. The stalls had clearly been carefully mended for
the white ponies, seven in all, who whinnied in their stalls
when they saw Saint George.

"Hello, my lovelies," he cooed back so unselfconsciously
that you could tell it was his customary greeting to them.

The stalls only took up about a third of the stable. The
rest was occupied by such an impressive collection of small
carriages that Lucia and Max both cried, "Whoa!" in uni-
son and rushed over to get a better look. There was a beautiful white phaeton with red velvet seats, and a black
carriage with a deep blue interior striped in gold. There
was a small maroon stagecoach with black shades that
rolled down, just like you'd see in an old cowboy movie,

and a white Cinderella pumpkin-shaped carriage with a round wrought-iron cage surrounding a pink circular seat. And of course there was the funeral carriage in which they had first travelled to the folly.

"Are these all yours?" Lucia called over to Saint George, who was harnessing up one of the ponies.

"They belonged to all us Kneebone kids originally," Saint George answered. "But when things went sour and we had to sell everything, my brother and sister wanted to sell the carriages, along with the ponies. I bought them out and kept them. What's he saying?"

Lucia looked over to see Otto's right hand twisting around the left then linking fingertip to fingertip.

"He wants to help," Lucia translated. "Let him. He's good with animals."

Saint George nodded toward the pony in the stall next door. "He can start harnessing Twinkle. But mind her ears, she doesn't like them fussed with."

"Twinkle!?" Lucia snorted, but that fetched such a grimace from Saint George that she shut up fast.

Twinkle was a fat-bellied and good-natured pony, all white like the others except for a star-shaped patch of beige on her neck. She stood patiently while Otto put the harness on her. Lucia stroked her beneath her muzzle. It was hypnotically silky, so that when Lucia felt the swipe of a dry, rough tongue, she jumped and yanked her hand away in surprise.

"Licked you, did she?" Saint George said, coming over and slapping Twinkle's shoulder affectionately. "She's part hound, this one. Licks and she chases rabbits and would sleep in your bed if you let her. Her mother was just the same, only not so fat. It's her in the shop's front window, you know." He said this last thing rather slyly.

"What? Do you mean the fake miniature zebra?" Max said.

"You knew she was fake?" Saint George said, surprised.

"Well, I mean . . . a *miniature zebra*?" Max said, shrugging.

"All right, but most people think she's real. Had lots of offers for her too. They couldn't pay me enough for old Beezy."

Lucia started to snort, "Beezy!" but thought better of it, and instead said, "She makes a good-looking zebra."

"She was a beauty," he said. "And smart. Charlie liked to hear about her."

"Charlie? Oh, The Kneebone Boy!" Max said. "Mr. Pickering said his name. Did you visit him in the tower a lot?"

"Yeah, quite a bit. My parents never knew. They didn't like us to see him. At first I used to go there with my brother and sister, but after a while I started to go on my own. They always stirred him up too much. He could stay calm and quiet if you knew how to talk to him. And since I was the only one who could get past the dragon, I snuck in pretty often. He liked to hear about the clever things Beezy did."

"Was he really a monster?" Lucia blurted out.

"Do you mean was he covered with hair and did he have claws and bat ears?" Saint George responded drily.

He shook his head. "Charlie was no monster. He was just put together all wrong, poor sod. I reckon he looked very peculiar, but I never noticed much. He was good company."

"Could he talk?" Lucia asked.

"Talk? No. Not like a regular person. He made sounds, the way an animal does, but we found a way to understand each other. Like the way you understand your brother here. He knew how to laugh though. I always wondered how he'd learned that. He didn't ever have much to laugh about, spending his life hidden away so that the rest of us Kneebones could live as though everything were just fine. I only wish I'd taken him out to the woods. I always promised him I would one day."

"Why didn't you?" Lucia asked.

"The arrow suddenly went missing and I couldn't get back into the passageway." Saint George's voice turned bitter. "I always suspected it was my brother and sister that did it out of spite. Threw it in the Abyss, did they? They were always jealous that I could get in on my own and they couldn't."

"What happened to Charlie?" Otto asked.

"He says, 'What happened to Charlie?'" Lucia translated.

"Died," Saint George answered simply. "At bloody seventeen years old. They all die young . . . The Kneebone Boys."

"We're sorry," Lucia said.

"Ah," he shrugged. "What can you do?" He adjusted

Twinkle's breast collar. "Strange thing happened a few months ago though. When I was out hunting, I saw this little twist of fog. It was hovering, like, between the trees. When I moved, it followed me. It seemed as if it were trying to play a game with me, hiding behind trees then sweeping around rocks and flying up into the branches. It followed me for a good half hour. If I believed in ghosts, I would have sworn it was Charlie himself, finally free and doing just as he pleased."

He scratched Twinkle's neck beneath her mane. "Anyway, I still have old Beezy. She dresses up the shop window nicely. And at Christmas I put a crown on her head and string her full of lights."

The Hardscrabbles nodded and pretended they didn't find that at all creepy.

The ponies were ready and Saint George started for the funeral carriage, but Lucia said, "Do you think we might go in one of the other carriages?"

There was a brief argument among the Hardscrabbles over which carriage to take until Saint George told them to shut their gobs or he'd make them walk while he took the carriage himself. Then he hitched the ponies to the handsome black one with the blue velvet seats, which incidentally was the one Lucia had wanted in the first place. Saint George even dug out a plaid wool blanket from an old chest to put over their laps. It smelled a little like mouse droppings but never mind.

It was heaven to ride in the carriage! The sultan's awful circumstances were not forgotten, but it was hard to feel weepy while racing through the woods in the middle of the night, your legs warm, if itchy, from the wool blanket and the wind trying to force your eyelids shut. Lucia's fingers traced the tiny square pillows quilted into the blue velvet seat and listened to the *creak-creak-creak* of the springs beneath. In a carriage, the night air feels exhilarating rather than just chilly, as it did when they were on foot, and the path was not long and dreary but breathtaking, especially as the carriage began to go downhill. Up front in the child-size driver's seat, Saint George hulked low, putting so much weight at the head of the carriage that when the road started to dip, the carriage seemed on the verge of flipping over itself. The Hardscrabbles had to brace their backs against the seat to keep from slipping forward until Saint George finally reined in the ponies and they slowed to a walk.

"Saint George," Lucia said, leaning forward when she suddenly thought of something. "Why did you tell me that it was The Kneebone Boy in the woods when you knew very well it wasn't?"

There was a long pause, so long that Lucia thought he didn't hear her. She was about to ask again, when he said, "Let's just say there aren't a lot of places in Snoring for wild critters to live, and a taxidermist needs wild critters."

"Needs to slaughter them, you mean," she said sharply.

"Whatever you like." Saint George shrugged. "Unfortunately, these woods don't belong to Kneebones anymore."

"Oh. So you were poaching then?"

Saint George didn't bother to answer her.

"Did you think telling us about The Kneebone Boy would scare us enough to keep out of your way?" Lucia asked.

"It would have if you lot were normal," he said.

"Well, we're not," Lucia said and sat back against the seat. "Not at all." It felt really good to say that, especially when other people had been saying that about them for so long.

The horses pulled into the clearing and Saint George brought them to a halt and jumped off the driver's seat.

"Right," he said. "Everyone out. If you don't want to wake up the neighbourhood, we'd better leave the carriage here and walk the rest of the way."

The horses were tied to a tree. Saint George and the Hardscrabbles cut across the stretch of meadow between Kneebone Castle and the folly. From their vantage point, they could only see the castle's uppermost windows, all of which were black except for one in the northern corner. Lucia thought it might be the one in which she had spotted a man at his desk while she stood on the siege tower, but she couldn't be sure. The ugly, misshapen castle had pulled up its drawbridge, like a great mouth that had slammed shut. *We have the sultan,* it seemed to say. *He's in here, in us.*

They crossed the folly's drawbridge, noting with relief that Haddie's bedroom light was still out. They slipped across the courtyard and into the folly as silently as possible. Max and Lucia went to the Great Hall with Saint George while Otto went down to the dungeon to fetch the arrow.

"So she's kept the heads up, has she?" Saint George said, nodding at the mounted deer heads approvingly. "That's my own handiwork."

"She's kept everything, I think," Max said. "She makes us toasted cheese sandwiches in the pink toy oven."

"Crazy American," he said, shaking his head. But still he looked pleased. He walked up to the grandfather clock, wrapped his arms around it, and moved it easily off to the side, exposing the little door behind it. Just the sight of it made Lucia and Max take a step backwards. Kneeling down, Saint George rapped on the door lightly with his fingertips. "Remember me, old mate?" he said quietly.

The Great Hall door opened and Otto appeared clutching the arrow in one hand with Chester at his heels. At the sight of the arrow, Saint George stood up slowly. He held out his hand, his fingers beckoning impatiently. Otto handed the arrow to him. Saint George turned it in his hands, examining its white feather fletches and its golden tip.

"That's her," he said, shaking his head in disbelief.

"Good," Lucia said. "Now we should get on with it, don't you think? It's nearly one o'clock."

"Right," Saint George said distractedly. Above the grandfather clock was the collection of archery bows. Reaching up, Saint George took one off its hook. He studied it, running his hand across the bow string, then put it back on the wall. He picked up another one and did the same thing. This one seemed like it would do. He walked back to the little door and crouched down.

"Stand back."

He didn't need to tell them that, incidentally.

He pressed the bone button and leapt backwards. The door flew open and instantly the dragon's head emerged, whipping its neck round and spraying out flames. They missed Saint George by a finger's width, he was that close. He must have known the exact limits of the dragon's reach because he stood his ground unflinchingly. Lifting his bow, he pulled the arrow back, his body still and his eyes following the wild movements of the dragon's head. But he didn't shoot. He stood like this for a very long time, poised to release the arrow without actually releasing it.

Lucia bent her head toward Max and whispered, "What's wrong?"

"Nothing. He just needs to wait for the right moment," Max whispered back.

The very next second, the arrow was launched. It sliced through the air and pierced the dragon's left eye with a sharp *tink* sound. The dragon shrieked. His head stopped whipping. It tipped up and its mouth belched a blast of fire before collapsing to the stone floor with a metallic crash.

"Oh, well done!" Lucia cried.

The Hardscrabbles walked up to the dragon and knelt beside it for a better look. It was made of thousands of tiny enameled metal scales, layered so that the head could bend easily. They pried open the jaws and saw a tiny metal pipe through which the fire had shot out. Its eyes, which had looked so alive and menacing just moments before, were now still and blank. Doll's eyes. The arrow was lodged snugly in its pupil, and as Max pulled it out, Lucia noticed a curious thing. The dragon's pupils were jagged, like the tip of the arrow. Max saw it too, and he moved the arrow in and out of the eye a few times, studying how they fit together.

"It's a key," Max said.

Saint George was watching them, and now he stuck out his hand out. "Give it here."

"Who made it?" Max asked, handing the arrow to him.

"My grandfather. Put in the dragon and built the secret passageway too. The man liked to make a game of everything. Came from growing up in the castle folly himself, I guess. Our father didn't want us to have the arrow. He knew it was the key to the passageway, and to The Kneebone Boy's room, and he didn't like us to have anything to do with Charlie. But our grandfather slipped the arrow to us anyway." He blew on the fletches. "Good to have it back."

"So can we go now?" Lucia asked eagerly.

Saint George stared at them all very seriously.

"Yes, yes, we know. It's no romp in a theme park," Lucia said.

"You'll manage the first part all right," he said. "A straight shot down the tunnel, then across a bridge. You'll have to be careful enough on the bridge, but the worst bit is after that. You've got to cross a ledge. You can't walk it. It's too narrow. You've got to cross it sideways, back to the wall. It's a long drop to the bottom so don't muck about.

You'll come to an opening in the cliff. Go inside and you'll find the stairs. Follow them up till you can't go any further—"

"And that's where you go through the fireplace," Lucia interrupted impatiently. "We know. Mr. Pickering told us."

"I still don't like it," Saint George said. "Your aunt should know what you're going to do."

"Maybe we *should* tell her," Max said.

Otto said something. He had to repeat it, because no one had been looking at him.

"She already knows," he said.

He pointed up at the coffered ceiling. Above their heads, streaming out of the helmet visor of a carved knight on horseback, was a shaft of light. Suddenly the light vanished and helmet visor went dark again.

"A spy hole," Lucia said.

"Brilliant!" Max said.

"I always wondered how our tutor knew we stuffed his car keys in the stag's ears," Saint George said, staring up at the ceiling.

They heard soft footsteps above their heads, and when they died away with no sign of Haddie appearing, Lucia shrugged and said to Saint George, "There. You see. She knows, and she doesn't mind."

Saint George grabbed the dragon's head and yanked it hard. Behind it, attached to the base of its neck, was yet another door, a bit smaller than the first one. It swung open revealing only a rectangle of blackness. The opening was so small that the Hardscrabbles had to get down on their hands and knees to crawl in. Once they were through, though, they could stand up very comfortably. Otto switched on the torch and they found that they were indeed in a narrow tunnel made of rough-hewn stones that arced low, just a little above Otto's head. It was chilly in the tunnel and the air smelled like no one had sniffed it in a very long time. Chester poked his head through the door, sneezed, and backed out into the Great Hall again. Maybe they should have taken that as a sign.

Otto shined the torch down the passage. It illuminated a long tunnel that gradually sloped downwards, stretching out so far that the beam of light faded before it could find a hint of an end. Lucia felt her heart beating in nervous little knocks. Since she was feeling fairly brave at the moment, she knew it was Otto's fear that was doing the knocking.

"All right?" she said to him.

"I wish I were back in Little Tunks now," he said.

"We'll be there tomorrow," Lucia replied, keeping her voice kind but firm. "And Little Tunks will be exactly the same as it was when we left it, and so will all the people there, but we won't be. We'll have done something heroic. We'll have rescued a sultan. Think, Otto. We may never get the chance to do something heroic again."

"What about sailing a full-rigged ship and navigating by the stars?" Otto said. "What about rescuing people on islands?"

"Don't you remember what Haddie said?" Lucia replied. "That people should have all their adventures before they're fourteen because if they don't they lose their passion for adventures? What if we get older and forget what it's like to want a big adventure? What if we become like all other grown-ups, only thinking about how much money we make every year and if we've remembered to lock the door at night? I couldn't bear it, Otto." She looked at his worried face. "All right?" she asked again.

The shadows cast from the beam of the torch made him look more careworn than a thirteen-year-old boy should. Maybe he's too old already, Lucia thought. Maybe he already slipped into that grown-up world when I wasn't noticing, and now it's too late.

Otto's elbows quickly bumped against each other. "All right."

"Good," she said under her breath, smiling. She grabbed his hand and squeezed it. It was icy cold, and it didn't squeeze back.

Chapter 21

In which Lucia wonders if Big Adventures
are all they're cracked up to be

The stones beneath their feet were slippery, and wearing trainers didn't help, so they moved along slowly. In the distance they could hear a hollow, quivering sound like the tail end of an echo.

"I wonder why Haddie let us go?" Lucia mused as they made their way through the tunnel. "She promised Dad she'd keep us out of trouble."

"I don't think Haddie likes rules," Max replied. "Even her own."

They turned round a snaky bend, their eyes squinting into the torch's beam to find the tunnel's end. There was only more darkness as far as the eye could see. There was nothing to do but walk and try not to think about rats.

"Imagine Haddie back at Little Tunks," Max said.

"We'd never have to stay with Mrs. Carnival again," Lucia said.

"Dad wouldn't always have that look about him."

The beam of light from the torch began to dance around so they glanced at Otto.

"Listen," he said.

They stood still and listened. At first they heard nothing, but soon there was the faintest scurrying sound.

"Rats probably," Max said.

"No, not really!?" Lucia said, horrified. Her bare legs instantly felt goose pimply and she quickened her pace.

The tunnel seemed to go on and on. It always takes forever to go places when you have never been there before, but when you are travelling subterraneously, with the expectation of rats underfoot, it can feel like an eternity. After a while, though, the passageway took another sharp turn. When they rounded it, they saw that the tunnel walls abruptly ended and opened out into nothing at all. A vista of black sky faced them. The ground dropped off, and the sound of water idly splashing against rocks far, far below warned them that they must be on a cliff.

Otto shone the torch around, and they spied a crooked stone bridge jutting out from the ledge, spanning the void between where they stood and another sheer cliff to the right. This cliff was taller than the one they stood on, and quite jagged with small bushes and stunted trees sprouting here and there in the crannies.

Lucia eyed the bridge warily. There were no handrails,

just a dizzying walk high above the sea. To fall off it would be massively unlucky.

"You can crawl across it," Max suggested when he saw her expression.

"Don't be ridiculous," Lucia said, although she had just been thinking that very same thing. But the way Max said it made her decide not to. "Well, Otto can if he wants," she added.

"My scarf would get caught," he said. "I'll walk it."

They did. No one fell.

Though there was one awful point where Otto lost his balance and had to crouch down for a moment and grab hold of the bridge. It was a horrifying few seconds for everyone involved so you'll understand if I just skip it.

Now that they had reached the other cliff, they could see that it was in fact the cliff that Kneebone Castle sat on. If they bent their necks back they could just make out the lumpy stones of the castle's keep. Mind you, they had to bend their heads back while their spines were pressed against the cliff face because they had come to the most dangerous part of the secret passageway. All that stood between them and the ocean below was a narrow ledge, about the width of your hand if you are over the age of nine and under the age of sixteen. If you press your hand against the bottom of your foot, you'll see just how narrow this ledge was.

Max was first in line, then Lucia, last of all Otto. Now Lucia truly could not tell the difference between Otto's thumping heart and her own.

"All right?" Max said, getting ready to move.

And to Lucia's own surprise she answered, "No. Not all right. Not even the smallest bit all right."

Otto said something then. Out of the corner of her eye, Lucia could see his hands moving, but she was too scared to turn her head to see what he was saying. Even looking at him sideways made her dizzy so she shut her eyes.

"He says—" Max started to translate, but then he stopped in confusion and asked Otto to repeat it.

"Right. He says," Max tried again, still sounding uncertain, "that 'if you look straight ahead, you can see the Orion constellation.'"

She didn't want to open her eyes. Still, after a few deep breaths, she forced herself to. There, dead ahead, was Orion's belt, the three bright stars each with its pale blue nimbus, surrounded by a cluster of pinprick stars. She had been so scared she hadn't noticed how curiously the sky encircled them. Where the sky bottomed out, the ocean took over, its black slick waves stretching out to the tail ends of the world in all directions. This must be how it feels to be on a ship, she thought.

Lucia had never had to try to imagine anything. Her mind just naturally slipped into stories, sometimes without her even knowing she'd done it. But now, when a single misstep would mean a tumbling plunge to her death, she had to try. A ship, a ship, she thought. I am on a ship.

No, you are on a cliff! her brain screamed back at her.

I'm on a fully rigged sailing ship, she thought, ignoring

her brain. I can even hear the waves crashing against the starboard side.

It's the cliff that the waves are crashing against!

Shut up, it's the starboard side, she told her brain. The weather's dirty tonight, lads, and the sea is a demon.

She felt Otto's hand grab hers. "But my crew is brave and my ship handles well in fair weather or foul."

Max grabbed her other hand. Then step by tiny step she began to move across the ledge, her eyes and her mind held steady by the sight of Orion's belt. Each step, she told herself, is one step closer to the sultan. One more, and one more, and—

"Nearly there," Max cooed.

They say that if you force yourself to laugh when you are feeling especially dismal, you will automatically feel cheerier about things. It's something to do with glands, I think. That night, Lucia discovered a similar remedy for fear. With her spine pressed straight against the wall and her chin tipped high so that her eyes could remain fixed on Orion, she assumed the universal pose of courage. And do you know, she began, ever so slowly, to feel more and more courageous. By the time she felt comfortable enough to let her mind wander (she was contemplating the sultan's face when he saw the Hardscrabbles burst into his room), the ledge began to widen. Max stopped. He let go of her hand.

"It's all right," he said. "We can walk normally now. Just stay close to the cliff."

Well, one doesn't quite walk "normally" while on the

243

edge of a precipice, but it was certainly an improvement. Before long they came to a fissure in the cliff, wide enough for a child or a smallish grown-up to slip through.

"This must be it," Max said. "Give us some light in there, Otto."

It looked like a cave at first glance but the torch found a set of crudely carved stairs along the back wall. The stairs rose up, through a vertical tunnel of stone, twisting round and round at a steep incline.

"Ready to climb?" Max said.

Lucia and Otto nodded. Up they went, Max at the lead, Lucia in the middle and Otto holding the torch upwards from his position at the bottom. The stairs were shallow and the space was tight. They had to press their hands against the walls for balance as they climbed. Round and round they went in the most dizzying way, higher and higher, until their thigh muscles felt like they'd been pummeled.

"How much longer to the tower, do you think?" Lucia asked, panting.

"The tower? I doubt we've reached the castle's dungeon yet," Max said, also breathless.

They continued on, with Otto staring up at Lucia's bum, Lucia staring up at Max's bum, and Max having the lucky bumless view. Suddenly the rock face changed. The stones were now the rough-cut lumps of the castle wall. Up close they were mud brown with red veins creeping across them, and they gave off the smell of long-buried coins.

"Okay, we're in the castle," Max whispered. There was

no reason to whisper really, but it did make them feel eerie to be inside. It was like travelling beneath the skin of a giant. The castle's stones even felt different from the cliff's rock. The stones were warmer beneath their hands, and there was a smoothness to the lumps, like great, clenched muscles. They could hear sounds now too, a faint humming from somewhere deep in the bowels of the castle and once, as they climbed higher, the sound of someone crying. That made them stop in their tracks until the crying ceased. Then, without a word to one another, they kept climbing. There was nothing else to do after all. Not really.

"There's something up ahead," Max whispered suddenly. "Here. Otto, pass me up the torch."

The torch was passed and Max shined it above his head, waving it this way and that.

"Bad," Max said finally.

"What? Bad *what*?" Lucia cried.

"They've built an extension," Max said.

It was a close thing. Lucia had even formed a fist and was about to make contact with the back of Max's thigh when Otto squeezed her ankle to keep her from doing it.

"That's not funny, Max!" she said. "Are you trying to give me a heart attack?"

"No, it's *not* funny," Max said. "Don't you understand? The extension blocks the stairs. Look."

Lucia climbed a little higher and gazed up. He was right. There was a narrow space between the wallboard and the stone wall but then it was blocked off altogether by wooden beams and, above that, solid wood planking.

"But how do we get to the sultan then?" Lucia said.

"I don't know," Max said.

At first she thought he was joking. Max always knew what to do next. She waited for him to say, "Never mind, just wanted to see you squirm. Here's what we do." And then he would tell them his brilliant idea.

But he didn't.

"Well, there must be something!" Lucia said. "We can't just turn back now."

"I don't see what else we *can* do," Max said.

They stood there, all three of them, not quite believing their bad luck and hating extensions in general and wondering bitterly, and out loud, why a castle as big as the Kneebone Castle would even need an extension to begin with.

It was Otto who surprised them and began to climb again. He squeezed past Lucia, then Max, grabbing the torch out of his hands.

"It's no use, Otto," Max said.

But Otto kept going until he came to the narrow space between the stone wall and the wallboard. With a hop, he pulled up his legs and pressed the soles of his trainers against the wallboard while pushing his back against the stone wall. Now off the ground, his body forming an L, he began to shimmy up the wall. He managed to shimmy all the way to the top of the wallboard wall before he could go no further.

"Come on down, Otto," Lucia said. "It's no good."

Instead of coming down, though, the torch light suddenly went out and Otto vanished in the darkness.

"Otto?" they called up blindly.

There was no answer. Of course.

Lucia felt the first stirrings of panic beginning to set in.

"Go, go!" she said, pushing at Max's leg.

They both hurried up the stairs as best as they could in pitch blackness. Max yelped suddenly, and Lucia cried out, "What is it?"

"Hit my head on the wallboard," he said.

Suddenly light shone above them, seemingly from nowhere, illuminating the narrow space. Otto was nowhere in sight but they could hear a soft knocking against the wall, on the inside.

"He's in!" Lucia said. "But how—? Oh, look, there are spaces between the beams. He slipped in through there."

"Well, who could see it from down below?" Max said sulkily.

"Otto did somehow," Lucia said.

"Lucky guess."

"Oh, budge up and let me pass if you're just going to stand here and whinge about it," Lucia said.

That made Max move. They both shimmied up the wall, just as Otto had done, and when they got to the top they squeezed between the beams. Max went headfirst, which was unfortunate because it was a long drop to the floor. Otto caught him seconds before he cracked his head open. Lucia turned on her stomach and put her feet through the opening, then lowered herself slowly. She dangled for a minute before she had the courage to let go. Otto caught her too.

Then they looked all around to see where they had landed.

Mr. Dupuis says that at the start of every chapter, the author must ask him- or herself this question: What's the most important message you want to convey to your readers here? I have thought about this quite a bit. I gave it a solid twenty minutes anyway, while I was waiting at the dentist's office and couldn't find a decent gossip magazine.

Here is my most important message to you:

All great adventures have moments that are really crap.

Chapter 22

In which there is a lot of toilet paper
and feminine thingamathings

The Hardscrabbles had landed in a room filled with toilets. It wasn't a restroom, not quite yet. There were stalls, but the stalls were empty. Six toilets sat at one end of the room, along with miscellaneous pipes and nuts and bolts. A mop and bucket stood in one corner and in the opposite corner were shelves with a dozen large packs of toilet paper, several bottles of hand soap and disinfectant and, not to be rude, also boxes of feminine thingamathings.

Otto discovered the bad news right away.

"The door is locked," he said as he turned the knob. So of course Max and Lucia had to try the door too and they confirmed that it was indeed locked.

There was more bad news.

"I don't think we'll be able to get back out through the beams, either," Max said. "It's too high up."

They spent the next half hour trying to balance toilets on top of one another in order to reach the beams, but you can't imagine how unstackable toilets are. They tried to stack up on one another's shoulders as well, but they couldn't quite reach even then. Finally, they had to admit the awful truth of their situation.

"We're well and truly trapped!" Otto said, looking very panicky.

"Now look," Lucia said, trying to keep her voice bright even though she felt nearly as panicky as Otto, "there'll be workers coming to put in the toilets, won't there? They'll probably be here in the morning, and then we can slip out and find the sultan."

"Remember when we had the roof mended back home?" Otto said. "The workers said they'd be there the first of June and they didn't show up till the end of August."

This was perfectly true. Poor Casper had cartons of soggy sketches because of it.

"Yes, but you're forgetting about the toilet paper, Otto," Lucia said. "They're going to need toilet paper."

"One thousand and one sheets to the roll," Max said glumly, holding up a package with 1,001 SHEETS TO THE ROLL! printed on it.

"Shut up please," Lucia said. "Anyway, we can always yell and bang on the door until someone opens it. And you're forgetting Haddie. She knows we went through the passage. If we don't come back, she'll come looking for us."

"In any case, we'll be caught," Max said. "And then who knows what they'll do with us?"

It certainly did seem grim. Otto collapsed on one of the toilets, rested his head against the wall and shut his eyes, though his hands moved.

"Wake me up when someone comes," he said.

Lucia and Max watched him for a moment. Suddenly they too felt the full effects of a sleepless night filled with danger and anxiety, and now hopelessness.

"Right," Lucia said. "If we have to spend the night, we might as well make ourselves at home."

With Max's help, she arranged the packages of toilet paper to form a mattress for all three of them to share. The packs of feminine thingamathings were used for pillows.

They all lay there on their backs for a while, listening to the silence.

"I *do* remember her," Otto said suddenly.

"Who do you remember?" Lucia asked. Her voice sounded wispy with exhaustion.

"Mum," Otto said.

"You do?" Max cried. He rose up on his elbow, making the toilet paper packages crackle. "Then why on earth have you always said you didn't?"

There was no answer.

"Otto?" Max nudged him sharply with his foot.

"Let him be," Lucia said when Otto rolled over on his side, with his back to them.

"I just don't see why he has to be so secretive about things," Max grumbled. A few minutes later, Max was snoring.

Lucia, however, was still wide awake. She couldn't put

her finger on it, but there was something about Otto's secretiveness that reminded her of The Kneebone Boy. Maybe it was because of what Saint George had said—that The Kneebone Boy had spent his life hidden away so that the rest of the Kneebones could live as though everything was just fine. What was it that Otto was keeping from them? What did he know? It was impossible to figure. Utterly maddening!

She closed her eyes and tried to force herself to sleep.

Believe it or not, lying on a bed of toilet paper is actually quite comfortable.

But it's a poor end for an adventure.

It wasn't just the fact that the Hardscrabbles had been given an opportunity to do something heroic, something really great and good, and they had botched it. It wasn't that they would most likely *never* be on the telly news or have a plaque made about them. It wasn't even that they had lost any chance of returning to Little Tunks "lurgy free."

What really pained Lucia was that she would never ever see the sultan's face again. He was forever lost to her. She wouldn't even be able to look at Casper's sketch of him. It would be too awful to see that half smile, and to know that she had failed him. She could no longer bear to see his beautiful eyes staring back at her, daring her to do something really interesting, and knowing that she had done it and it had gone terribly wrong and that was the end of it.

She decided she would take the sketch down immediately when she returned home.

Then she turned her head away from her brothers and cried into a package of feminine thingamathings.

They slept well into the morning. There were no windows in the room and none of the Hardscrabbles wore a watch, so they woke up to Max's groan. "Cor, what time is it?"

"Late, I think. It feels late," Lucia groaned back and turned over to face him.

"What happened to *you*?" Max said. "Have you been crying? You look all ugly."

"Oh, thank you very much, you ought to smell your own breath." She turned away from him again and tried to dig out the crusty bits in her swollen eyes.

"What?" she heard Max say to Otto. "Oh, yeah, me as well."

"You as well what?" Lucia turned to see Otto sitting up and looking all uneasy.

"Oh, no," she said, shaking her head. "No, no, no! You can't."

"But the room is silly with toilets," Otto said.

"Toilets with no plumbing," Lucia said. "It's the same as peeing in a bucket. I won't sit in a room with pee strewn about."

"We don't strew," Max said.

"Don't you have to go too?" Otto asked her.

"Of course I do. But I have self-control."

That was equivalent to a dare, so they held it as long as they could. Which was about six minutes, give or take. They found that the toilets all had holes in the bottom so the boys peed in the bucket in the corner of the room. They took the mop out of the bucket first.

It is nearly impossible to hold it in when everyone else is peeing in a bucket, so Lucia did too.

Now you know the worst.

Well, nearly the worst.

A few minutes later, they heard a key in the door. I am proud to say they did not try to hide. There was nowhere to hide in any case, but they didn't even try. They stood there waiting for the next bad thing to happen. They knew that it might be very bad indeed, since the people who held the sultan were clearly not the best sort of people. And it would be *very* difficult to explain how they had wound up in the room without incriminating themselves.

Otto's hands started moving.

"Don't say a word," he said.

Which is sort of funny, coming from him. But that's hindsight because it didn't seem funny at the time; it seemed like good advice. The door was opened by a stout woman dressed in a pale blue uniform. She had been chewing gum when she opened the door but when she saw the Hardscrabbles standing dead center in the room, she stopped chewing. Her mouth remained open with lower jaw cocked to one side.

"Bloody hell, who are you?" she finally said.

The Hardscrabbles didn't say a word.

"How did you get in here?" she asked.

Again, not a word.

"Who do you belong to?"

You would think that deliberately not speaking is the easiest thing in the world. It's quite hard, actually. When someone asks, your natural urge is to answer, even if the answer is a lie. Lucia and Max instantly formed a new respect for Otto.

"All right," the woman said, her voice turning severe, "I'm locking you back in here while I go fetch someone to deal with you." She started to leave when Lucia called out, "Wait!"

The idea came to her in the form of a face, narrow and fine boned, with skin the color of cherrywood and nostrils that flared indignantly. The face of Princess Uzima, who had slept beneath a baobab tree on the African plains, appeared to Lucia clearly now. She felt the princess's beautiful, clever eyes fix on her own, and remembered Casper's words: "The Princess Uzima had nothing . . . no home, no money. Just her own wits and a vial of poison around her neck. But if she commanded a lion to sit up and beg, it would, because she was every inch a princess, down to her small toe."

Lucia threw back her shoulders, flared her nostrils, and said to the woman in the blue uniform, "You must take us to see the Sultan of Juwi."

The woman jerked her head backwards as though someone had unexpectedly flung something at her.

"The sultan! How do you know about the sultan?" she said.

"It doesn't matter," Lucia said. She felt her brothers' eyes on her, but she couldn't make out their expressions peripherally, and anyway the Princess Uzima would not have cared what anyone else thought. "The point is," she continued, "we've come a long way at tremendous personal risk, and we've had to do things that we would rather not have done"—she was thinking here about the bucket in the corner—"and we did it for the sultan's sake. Now please, would you kindly show us the way to his tower room?"

There was a long pause, during which the woman scrutinized all their faces. She chewed on her gum two times then stopped and said, "What are your names?"

"Lucia, Otto, and Max Hardscrabble," Lucia said. Then she added, "Of Little Tunks," because it sounded more official.

"Hardscrabbles," the woman said, nodding slowly, as though the name were significant, which was exactly what Lucia wanted her to think. "Does Dr. Azziz know you're here?"

"No, but Haddie does," Max said, finally speaking up. "She lives in the folly across the way. And Saint George, he—"

"Oh, for goodness' sake, shut it," Lucia said. Max always told too much.

The woman glanced behind her out the door, then said whispered. "All right. I'll do it for the sultan's sake. But if you get caught . . . that is, *when* you get caught, because you absolutely will, you had better not mention me."

"Of course not," Lucia assured her.

"And I won't speak up on your behalf either," she warned. "You're on your own."

"We're not afraid," Lucia said, feeling the Princess Uzima's long elegant arm wrap around her waist in approval.

"You say that now," the woman replied dryly. Her eyes suddenly flitted over to the corner of the room, where the bucket of pee stood. She stared at it, then looked back at the Hardscrabbles with raised eyebrows.

Now *that* was the worst.

Chapter 23

In which Lucia's hippocampus is nudged

She led them out of the room, down a winding hallway with a white marble floor and an arched ceiling, painted with scenes from Greek mythology. The hallway led into a large round vestibule with other hallways branching off in all directions and a massive set of stairs in the center.

"This way," the woman said briskly, starting up the stairs.

But just as Max and Lucia began to follow, Otto reached out quickly and grabbed their arms to stop them. When they turned, he put a finger to his lips. Then he said, "We won't find The Kneebone Boy up there."

"Where, then?" Lucia asked, using Otto's sign language.

Otto paused. He looked around the vestibule, his pale eyes flitting from hallway to hallway. There were five in all.

"That one," Otto said, pointing to the narrowest hall-way to the immediate left of the stairs.

"What's the matter?" The woman had realized that the Hardscrabbles were not behind her and was now glowering down at them from the stairs. "Come along, I haven't got all day."

"Leg it!" Max cried.

They dashed toward the narrowest hallway on the instant. They had seen Otto find so many hidden things in the course of their lives, that it never even occurred to them he might be wrong this time.

"Hey!" the woman shrieked after them. They heard her footsteps clapping heavily down the stairs, so they ran even faster. Otto was in the lead, wending through the hallway. They turned off at a juncture and flew down yet another hallway, past three tall windows that looked out toward the sea, then through a pair of double doors, whereupon they stopped and looked around in surprise.

They were in a courtyard, open to the sky and surrounded on all sides by a high stone wall. Cobblestone walkways meandered through the courtyard, swaddled by flower beds and young trees in boxes, giving a little shade to several long tables with benches beside them. A small fountain stood at the center of the courtyard with a sculpted angel in the center of it.

It was so wonderful to feel the sun on their necks after their journey through the murky tunnel and their night imprisoned in the restroom that they stood there for a moment, with their faces raised to the sky.

"Lovely day, Chippy, yeah?" a voice said.

The Hardscrabbles turned in alarm and spotted a very fat man sitting at one of the tables, watching them. His head was lowered and cocked to one side, the way people peek at something beneath their curtains when they don't want to be seen themselves. On the table in front of him was a plate on a tray, with a large sandwich, two glasses of milk, and an apple.

"Yes, very nice day," Max said nervously. The Hardscrabbles all wondered if this was Dr. Azziz. They waited, frozen where they stood, to see what he would do next.

The man turned his head away so that he appeared to be looking over his right shoulder. "No Harriet about today, yeah?" he said. "We're safe as houses, Chippy. Nothing to worry about."

This was rather confusing.

"Who's Harriet?" Max asked.

The man didn't answer. He only plucked off a corner of his sandwich and placed it on his right shoulder.

The Hardscrabbles were baffled but not quite as scared anymore. The large man seemed in no hurry to sound an alarm. He didn't even seem particularly curious about where they had come from. He just stared at his right shoulder, occasionally wiggling his fingers at it.

"Oh, look!" Max said. "He has a little mouse on his shoulder."

The others looked and saw it too—a little black mouse that was sitting on its tiny haunches, holding a bit of sandwich between its paws and nibbling on it.

260

The man looked at the Hardscrabbles in his behind-the-curtain way. Then he put out one finger toward the mouse and the little thing scampered onto it, gripping it tightly as the man brought his finger down to the table. With a leap, the mouse jumped down and stared up brightly at the Hardscrabbles.

"Kill the spider, yeah?" the man said, and he wiggled his pudgy fingers in front of the mouse. The mouse lunged at the man's fingers and batted at them with his tiny paws.

"Oh, he's clever!" Lucia said. Otto crouched down in front of the table to look at the mouse eye to eye.

"Ride on the horse, Chippy," the man said, pressing his fingertips against the table and cupping his hand above it. Nimbly, the mouse leapt onto the man's hand and held on while the hand pretended to trot, then gallop, then rear up.

"Revolting!" a woman's voice came from behind them. The man quickly scooped up his mouse and held him under the table. The Hardscrabbles turned to see that two women had entered the courtyard. One had the sort of curly blond hair you see on a toddler, but she was probably close to fifty years old. The other woman was much younger and was tall, slim, and terribly pale. Her hair was pale too, almost pink, and it was pulled back in a long, limp ponytail. She held a tray with two sandwiches on them and two cups of coffee.

"There's a rule about rodents, Frank!" The curly-haired, blond woman stormed up to the man and smashed a fist down on the table. "*That's* what I do if I see that thing on the table again. Squash! *That's* what I do!" She looked at the Hardscrabbles now, noticing them for the first time.

"Do you have any rodents in your pocket?" she demanded. It was hard to know which Hardscrabble she was talking to because one of her eyes was going in the wrong direction.

"Harriet, please, let them alone, you're scaring them," the other woman said in a soft voice. "Come, we'll sit way over there. The mouse won't come close, dear." She spoke to Harriet so gently and sweetly, just like a very patient mother would speak to an unreasonable child. Harriet grumbled but she followed the younger woman to a table at the far end of the courtyard.

Now it began to occur to Max and Lucia that Otto may have been gravely mistaken. The sultan was nowhere to be seen. Other people began to come into the courtyard now. Who *were* all these people? Lucia wondered. They carried trays of food and paper cups of coffee or tea and they sat down at the tables and stared at the Hardscrabbles. Lucia stared back. Something was nudging at her hippocampus. I just learned this word in biology and it is especially excellent because it sounds like it might be rude, as in "Move your big fat hippocampus" whereas it actually means the part of your brain that helps you remember things.

"Excuse me," Lucia said to the man with the mouse, "do you know where the sultan is?"

The man looked at her sideways, his mouse still cupped in his lap, but he didn't answer.

262

"I said, do you know—" Lucia started to repeat but was interrupted by the sight of a black woman with her hair bound back by a yellow headscarf approaching the table very briskly with a heaping tray of food in her hands.

Lucia once again felt a nudge at her hippocampus.

The woman in the yellow headscarf stopped when she noticed the Hardscrabbles. "Who are *they*?" she asked the man with a cool, nod towards the Hardscrabbles.

"They want the sultan," the man with the mouse muttered. Then he looked off to the right very suddenly as if someone else had said that and he was wondering who.

"The sultan? The sultan's right over there," she said, jerking her head toward the door before she sat down at the table with the man.

The Hardscrabbles turned and there, indeed, was the sultan in his white robe, entering the courtyard. In the bright daylight he seemed more fragile and yet more handsome than when Lucia had seen him in the woods. The light seemed to peekaboo through his skin, like sun through a seashell. His robe was sadly shredded and soiled around the bottom, Lucia could now see, and without his bejewelled mustard-lid crown from the sketch he looked like a rumpled teenager who had just woken up. Tucking his hands into the sleeves of his robe, he turned down one of the little paths, lifting his face to the sun, just as the Hardscrabbles had done when they first entered the courtyard. When he reached the fountain he hitched up his robe and stepped right in, sloshing through the shallow water, then stepped up onto the pedestal, and again up on the angel's stone feet, bare like his own. He climbed up onto the angel's shoulder and sat down on its curly head with his feet resting on the tipped water-jug spout. From out of his robe pocket he pulled a peeled hard-boiled egg. Then he looked out at the people in the courtyard and smiled.

Mr. Dupuis says, "Writers should avoid clichés like the plague." He says that one way to tell if a phrase is overused is if you have heard it in an advertisement. For instance, the Drift-Away mattress company swears they will make you "sleep like a baby." And "not a happy bunny" is what the announcer says in the telly ad when the kid snaps off the head of Gromley's Chocolate Easter Bunny. The Such Fun Chewing Gum company promises that their gum will give you a "dazzling smile," so I suppose it is a cliché, but the thing is, the sultan's smile *was* dazzling. It was the sort of smile that made you smile back before you even knew what you were doing. The sultan raised his egg in the air and the others in the courtyard raised their paper cups or their sandwiches or their forkfuls of salad.

"Cheers, m'dears!" the sultan called out.

"Cheers!" the others called or murmured or, in the case of the man with the mouse, simply mouthed silently with a sideways look.

It was then, while Lucia was gazing around the courtyard, that she realized why her hippocampus was being nudged. Her eyes went wide and she sucked in her breath.

"What is it?" Max asked.

"It's *them*!" Lucia said under her breath. "All of them!"

"Them what?" Max asked.

"Look around! Look! *Look!*" Lucia cried. "We've seen them all before."

"Lucia, get a grip," Max said. "You're imagining things."

"Shut up, and yes, we *have* seen them before," Lucia said. She glanced at Otto but he was mesmerized by the sultan.

"Look, Max," Lucia said, looping her arm through Max's and pulling him close so as to whisper in his ear. "Look really carefully. They're all here."

She pointed at the gloomy, handsome young man who leaned lethargically against a tree, sipping a cup of tea. "Prince Wiri. The one whose family was suspected of witchcraft. And Harriet, the woman with the curls—" Harriet was dipping the corner of her sandwich into her coffee while the young woman with the pale hair read the newspaper out loud to her. "Look at her wonky eye. It's the Duchess of Hildenhausen. She doesn't have the cornflowers in her hair but apart from that she's exactly like her. And the woman sitting with her, the one with the long blond hair, you've seen her face, Max, come on, you know you have. *Look* at her, for heaven's sake."

He looked at her. He looked at her for a full minute, which really is quite a good long time to look at someone whom you don't know, and finally he saw her.

"Empress Amalie of Schwartzenstadt-Russeldorf," he said very quietly.

"Yes!" Lucia said, barely able to keep herself from

squealing. "And this man here, with the lovely mouse. I had to think about it, because he has a beard in the sketch and he doesn't now"—the man was listening sideways—"but it's Prince Andrei and his black fox, only it's a mouse not a fox, but he does tricks just like the fox did."

"But I don't understand," Max said. "Does Dr. Azziz keep them all here against their will?"

"He keeps some of us against our will," said the black woman with the yellow headscarf. She had been watching them with interest as she chewed on her sandwich. "Others of us choose to stay."

Lucia gawked at her. She couldn't help it. Although Princess Uzima's hair was carelessly bound back and she was dressed in a plain navy blue T-shirt and jeans, she seemed only a hairsbreadth away from daring a lion to scrape its teeth against her splendid throat.

"We're all quite insane, of course," Princess Uzima continued, "but some of us are still sensible enough to realize it. Go." She waggled her long cherrywood fingers in the direction of the fountain. "Your sultan is waiting."

They obeyed, walking uncertainly up the stone path toward the fountain. They had counted on being the heroes, sweeping in, much to the sultan's joy, and setting him free. But now they found themselves perplexed and nervous and unsure what it was they had actually done.

When the sultan spotted them his smile evaporated. He chewed once in order to swallow his bite of egg, then swiped his lips with the back of his hand and dropped his egg into the stone angel's lap. He climbed down, more soberly than when he had leapt up, and walked through the fountain's pool once again, not bothering to lift his robe now. He stepped onto the path, looking at them, one at a time, with wonder in his eyes. For a good minute or two he said nothing at all. Then finally he spoke in his clear voice:

"I once had four advisors, all wise and good. They loved me and I loved them back. But of these four advisors, there were three whom I thought I'd never see again. Or if I ever did see them, I wouldn't know them and they wouldn't know me. So I gave one of them something of mine."

The sultan reached out with his slender fingers. His right hand had a curious spray of freckles on its knuckle that from their angle looked uncannily like a dog with floppy ears. Slowly, the sultan began to untie Otto's scarf. Lucia and Max stiffened, ready for something awful to happen, but Otto stood there calmly. He even lifted his chin to make it easier for the knot to come undone and in a moment the scarf was removed. Lucia and Max looked away. It was the same courtesy you would give to a person who has just had their hospital bandages taken off.

With a flick of his wrist, the sultan snapped the scarf in the air so that it made a popping sound and smoothed its folds. Then he—no, I'll say *she* now, because you have probably guessed that the sultan was none other than their mum, Tess Hardscrabble—wrapped it around her waist and tied it over her white robe. And there it was— the sultan's old mourning sash—the very one that Lucia had seen thousands of time in the sketch hanging on her bedroom wall, cinched around the sultan's waist. The very sash their father said had been left behind when the sultan disappeared.

"My fourth advisor," Tess Hardscrabble said, "is in London. I had to send him there on urgent business this week. He's having my crown mended."

At that moment, the courtyard door opened and Casper Hardscrabble entered, carrying a pale yellow hatbox with a white ribbon on top.

It's just in time too. He has a lot of explaining to do.

Chapter 24

In which Casper explains

Dr. Azziz was short and dumpy. He had very pretty white teeth and apart from pockmarked skin—which always looks so sinister but, if you think about it, simply means that the person was probably a very spotty, unattractive teenager—he was not the slightest bit terrifying. He arrived in the courtyard soon after Casper, tipped off by a nurse who had spied the Hardscrabbles. Dr. Azziz had looked at the stunned and confused face of Casper and then at the confused and stunned faces of the Hardscrabble children.

"Would you like a nice, quiet place to chat with the children, Mr. Hardscrabble?" he asked.

Dr. Azziz recognized a giant muddle when he spotted one, and giant muddles are best tackled in nice, quiet places.

"Yes, that's probably a good idea," Mr. Hardscrabble said faintly. He turned to his wife and handed her the hatbox. Then he bowed.

"Excuse me, Your Highness," he told her, "but with your permission I need to confer with . . . with the other advisors just now."

Tess Hardscrabble waved away his appeal. "Of course, I understand." She turned her eyes on her children and smiled so sweetly at them that they wanted to run straight into her arms. Max was the only one who actually did, though. He threw his arms around her waist and pressed his head against her chest. She just stood there, her arms at her side, not moving.

If you don't hug him back, Mum, Lucia thought, I will hate you forever, I will hate you forever, I will hate you forever!

Tess's arms slowly lifted and then, as though she were afraid she would hurt him, she gently wrapped them around her youngest child. A tiny sigh came from Casper, but whether it was of relief or sadness or joy, no one will ever know.

They stayed that way for a long time until Tess finally drew back, her hand stroking Max's hair (oh, Lucia remembered how wonderful that felt!).

"You will all come back and visit me again," Tess told them. "This palace is not as luxurious as the palace at Juwi, of course. The gardens are not so large, the views are not so beautiful. And of course, there are no peacocks. You do remember my peacock, don't you?"

Otto, Lucia, and Max all nodded.

Tess smiled again, satisfied. Then she turned and stepped back into the fountain, climbing the angel to the tippy-top and grabbing her egg on the way.

The Hardscrabbles followed Dr. Azziz into the hallway and up three sets of stairs to his office. It was all lovely with caramel-coloured walls and chocolate-coloured armchairs and a huge messy desk. Dr. Azziz offered Casper his desk chair and Otto, Lucia, and Max sat in the chocolaty chairs.

"Before I leave," Dr. Azziz said, "I would love to know how you children managed to sneak into the castle."

They told him. They didn't need to exaggerate a single thing, either. At the end Dr. Azziz whistled in appreciation.

"Extraordinary," he said.

Casper, however, was not so impressed. He had regained his composure somewhat, and now his eyebrows mashed together as he said, "I can't believe Haddie let you go. That was completely irresponsible of her."

"She didn't know that we were going," Max said, which we all know is a bold-faced lie, including Casper.

"She most certainly did!" Casper shot back. "When I arrived this morning and asked her where you all were, she told me you were 'storming the castle.' Called you her 'brave knights,' or some such rubbish. I honestly think the woman is completely mental."

Considering that they were sitting in the Snoring-by-the-Sea Psychiatric Hospital (they found that out later,

271

of course), this was probably not a stellar choice of words. Still, Dr. Azziz patted Casper on the shoulder, smiling very kindly.

"Well, it's all come out right in the end, Mr. Hardscrabble," Dr. Azziz said brightly. "Let's focus on that."

He left them alone then. For a full minute there was utter silence in the room. No one knew where to begin. It was Lucia who asked the first question.

"So has Mum been here the whole time, ever since she went missing?"

Casper stared down at his fingers, which were nervously rolling a pen back and forth on the desk. "Well . . . not the whole time. When she first went missing, I honestly didn't know where she was. She was just . . . I woke up one morning and she was gone. It was awful. My heart shattered into a thousand pieces that morning." He looked up at them for a moment, as if he were worried that what he'd said was too personal, before looking down at the pen again. "I looked everywhere for her. I was terrified she had done something violent to herself. I knew she wasn't well, even back then, though I tried not to admit it. When I couldn't find her on my own, I hired a private investigator and he was the one who finally found her. She was sitting at the top of a fountain in Regent's Park in London, telling passersby that she was the Sultan of Juwi. I brought her to different hospitals—good hospitals with good reputations—but she was miserable at all of them. They pumped her body full of medication. They tried to convince her that she was Tess Hardscrabble, not a sultan. I did too.

I wanted my Tess back so badly. I still do." He pressed his hand against his mouth for a moment before going on.

"Then I heard about this hospital. It seemed like the right place for her. A place where they'd let her be who she felt she was—the Sultan of Juwi." Casper looked up at his children as if to gauge their reaction.

"Does she know who we are?" Max asked after a moment.

Casper thought about this before he answered. "It's hard to say. I believe she knows that she loves us. And today, when she was with you three, there was something in her eyes so like the old Tess that I nearly . . ." He shook his head quickly as if to rid himself of a thought. "No, Max. I don't think she *really* knows who we are."

"And all the other people . . . the patients in the courtyard," Lucia said. "Why did you tell us they were royals?"

"So you knew the Duchess of Hildenhausen was Harriet, did you?" he said. He was clearly more chuffed than embarrassed about the lie. "Well, the funny eye gave it away, I suppose. But Prince Alexei? Without his beard even. I suppose the likeness was quite good . . ." He stopped smiling when he saw his children's solemn faces staring back.

"Yes, well." Casper cleared his throat. "All those times I went to visit your mum . . . well I had to explain it somehow, didn't I? And painting royal portraits seemed like such a beautiful lie."

"But it was *all* a lie," Lucia said angrily. "Why? Why did you hide the truth about Mum all these years? It wasn't fair, Dad, it wasn't right."

This, of course, was the question that Casper had been dreading and the one he knew that his children would, one day, ask him. He'd never imagined that the day would come so soon, though.

"I kept meaning to tell you . . . ," he stammered.

"Well, what good is *that*?" Max stormed at him. "All this time we might have known her. We might have visited her. We might have—"

"Did *you* know?" Lucia asked Otto suddenly.

They all looked at Otto, including Casper.

Otto said nothing at first. Then slowly, hesitantly, his hands began to move. "I didn't know where she was. But I knew there was something wrong with her. I remember when she began to change. All the strange things she did and said. And then she'd become herself again for a while, so you'd think you had imagined it all."

"*Did* he know?" Casper looked to Lucia for a translation. "I was never sure."

Otto nodded at his father and Casper buried his head in his hands.

"It was massively wrong of you to keep it from us, Dad!" Lucia said.

"I know."

"Beastly selfish!"

"I know it was," Casper groaned miserably. "Every year I'd say to myself, this is the year I'll tell them. They're old enough now. They can surely handle it. But just as I was about to sit you all down and tell you, I'd always become afraid that if I did . . . if I told you . . ." He stared at them helplessly, at a loss for words.

Ironically, it was Otto who found the words for him:

"He was afraid that if he told us about Mum, it would have made it all true."

The Hardscrabble children have many faults, I don't have to tell you that. But they have several very fine qualities as well and one of them is that they have a deep appreciation of how frail all human beings are, especially when it comes to the people they love. Also, they nearly always try to avoid stepping on ants when they can help it and they hardly ever drink straight from the milk container.

"I suppose we understand," Lucia said.

"Really?" Casper looked at all his children.

They all nodded, and Casper shook his head in wonder that such a gigantic muddle could have turned out so well, all things considered.

Right at this moment I could make a very happy ending. Mr. Dupuis says that it's best to end on a happy note.

Still it feels like there is more to say so I think I'll just carry on a little longer. Anyway, I am beginning to question if Mr. Dupuis really knows what he's talking about. I don't believe he's ever written a book, he only reads them, and writing them and reading them are very different things as I've come to find out.

✦ ✦ ✦

"Look at the time," Casper said, checking his watch. "We'll have to get started if we're going to catch the two-fifteen train."

"The train?" Lucia said, feeling suddenly quite deflated. "Back to Little Tunks you mean?"

"Well, where else?" Casper said.

"I don't know . . . ," Lucia said, frowning. "It just feels too soon. It feels like . . ."

"Like something more should happen," Max finished for her.

"And what about Haddie? We have to say good-bye to her at least," Lucia said.

"Oh, right. Haddie." Casper sighed, as if just saying her name exhausted him, and he reluctantly pulled an envelope out of his jacket pocket. "She asked me to give you this. I hate to think what it says. She's an odd one, that Haddie."

"Good odd," Lucia said as she reached for the envelope. Otto got it first though and he tore open the envelope, which was carefully sealed. The letter inside was written on the same light blue paper as her letter to Casper had been. The Hardscrabble children pulled their chairs close together and read it. Here is what it said:

Dear Otto, Lucia, and Max,
in no particular order,

Congratulations! If you are reading this it means that you are not dead, decapitated, or otherwise mortally wounded. It also means that you have probably met your mother. She's terrific, isn't she? Yes, I know she's mad as a hatter but she is still the most dazzling person I've ever known. And somewhere deep, deep down, she remembers all three of you. Why else would she have slipped out of the hospital when she spotted Lucia and Max on the siege tower (I was positive you'd go up there when I expressly told you not to. I would have done exactly the same and we are related after all)?

Now listen, there's nothing I hate more than weepy good-byes, so don't bother coming back to the folly because I won't be there. But I did want to tell you this. You might be feeling disappointed right about now because you have faced dark tunnels and high cliffs and grave danger, yet nothing has changed. You are still the Hard-scrabble kids who live in Little Tunks with their dad and not their mom. Though you have risked life and limb, you still have to clip your toenails every so often. Your lives will feel pretty blechhy for a while. All heroes feel that way after their adventure is over. But not to worry. You've had a big adventure before the age of fourteen, and now your lives will never be the same. Adventure is addictive, my friends. Before long you'll find some other way to risk your necks. Poor old Casper!

This won't be the last time we see each other (again, poor old Casper!). I have become very fond of the folly and Snoring-by-the-Sea and even of Saint George (we shared five packages of strawberry Twizzlers and seven packages of Ring Dings while we were waiting for your return. I even got him to eat a peanut butter and jelly sandwich and he didn't gag but I think he was just being brave). I plan on renting the folly at Christmas and again next summer and you can stay as long as you like. The Sultan of Juwi would be overjoyed. So would I.

You will find Chester in a cat carrier at the train station, being tended to by the guy at the ticket booth, who was feeding him salt-and-vinegar crisps last I saw. So heads-up for some unpleasant smells on the way back to Little Tunks.

With love and great admiration,
Great-aunt Haddie.

So, I guess this story's ending is what they call "bittersweet." In other words, things did not turn out the way the way the Hardscrabbles had hoped they would, yet somehow it all came out right anyway. Which I rather suspect is how life works in general.

As the train pulled away from the Snoring-by-the-Sea station, the Hardscrabbles stared out the window, watching as the view retraced their visit. They could see the path they had first walked towards the town. They caught a distant glimpse of the clutter of rooftops and the neighbourhood where they had found Saint George's shop. Finally they saw the familiar stretch of woods, thick, leafy hummocks that slipped downwards toward the valley.

It was Otto who spied it first. He suddenly leaned across Max and placed a finger on the window.

"Look!" he said.

"What?" Max asked.

"Don't you see it? Floating above the trees?"

"Do you mean that little cloud thing?" Lucia asked.

Otto shook his head. "It's not a cloud. It's fog." His hand automatically moved to touch his scarf before he remembered it was no longer there. Instead, he touched his neck. His hand lingered there for a moment, as though astonished at the feel of his own bare skin. "It's a little twist of fog," he said.

And that's exactly what it was. They watched it as it playfully tumbled over the treetops, diving down then reappearing a moment later, only to wind through the branches. They watched it until the train sped around a bend and it was lost from view.

So there is your one ghost, which I promised you back in Chapter Eleven.

I think I'm going to end this book here because the Hardscrabbles are all feeling quite wonderful now and in another twenty-four minutes they are going to have an argument over the windowseat on the train, during which things will get ugly.

Acknowledgments

I t's not that the Hardscrabbles are ungrateful. It's just that they are no good at this thank-you business, so they have handed the job over to Ellen Potter, who has loads of people she wants to thank and is not embarrassed to get soppy about it. Here she goes:

Thanks forever and always to my husband, Adam, who has been my best friend and champion since we were seventeen years old. Also a million thanks to my dear friend Anne Mazer, who, like Saint George, always hits the target, on and off the page.

I feel especially indebted to my brilliant editor, Jean Feiwel, who understands that a writer's favorite words are, "Write what you want to write. I trust you."

Thanks to my extraordinary agent, Alice Tasman, who

is just the sort of grown-up that the Hardscrabbles like best.

I am tremendously grateful to Liz Szabla, Dave Barrett, and Kathryn McKeon, who painstakingly nipped and tucked this manuscript into shape.

There are several people who helped massively with the writing of this book: Thanks to my young advisor and friend, Juwairiyya Asmal-Lee, who is as bold and funny and honest as Lucia Hardscrabble. Thanks to fellow writer and friend Sumayya Lee, who generously vetted this book. Also I am very grateful to Dayna Nye and John Swartz for their updates on gits, lurgies, and all manner of sugary snacks.